IN SEARCH OF HONOR

by Donna Lynn Hess

Bob Jones University Press, Greenville, South Carolina 29614

Library of Congress Cataloging-in-Publication Data:

Hess, Donna Lynn, 1952-
In search of honor / by Donna Lynn Hess

Summary: Fourteen-year-old Jacques Chénier is drawn into the tumult of the French Revolution as he struggles to free himself from the prison of his own bitterness and find the true meaning of honor.
ISBN 0-89084-595-6
1. France—History—Revolution, 1789-1799—Juvenile Fiction. [1. France—History—Revolution, 1789-1799—Fiction. 2. Christian life—Fiction.] I. Title.
PZ7.H4327In 1991
[Fic]—dc20 91-26926
CIP
AC

In Search of Honor

Edited by Brenda Thompson Schoolfield

Graphics by Kathryn L. Bell

Cover: *Prise de la Bastille le 14 juillet 1789. Arrestation du Gouverneur, Monsieur de Launay.* ©Réunion des Musées Nationaux.

Greenville, South Carolina 29614

Printed in the United States of America

ISBN 0-89084-595-6

20 19 18 17 16 15 14 13 12 11 10 9

For Elaine Fremont
Proverbs 27:17

PUBLISHER'S NOTE

It is the year 1787, and Paris is already beginning to experience the upheaval of the French Revolution. Angry peasants shout their grievances, and impassioned politicians cry their opinions; but the riots, rebellions, and violence still lie ahead.

The chaos of the Revolution has not yet reached the family of Jacques Chénier, fourteen, who lives in the St. Antoine neighborhood of Paris. His father is an artist, a talented sculptor. His mother makes lace and sells it to the nobility. But their peaceful existence is shattered in one terrible moment, and Jacques is left with a heart filled with bitterness. On his solitary walks through Paris, it seems to him that the river Seine reflects both the serenity that he cannot attain and the fitful waves of circumstance that have swept him to disgrace.

His bitterness deepens into self-loathing as he is caught up in the turmoil of the Revolution, but Jacques comes at last to understand the truth of his new friend's words: *"It is the heart, not the circumstances, that determines whether we are men of honor or disgrace."*

The book begins with Jacques's own introduction to the story of his search for honor.

1. Jacques' neighborhood
2. Charpentier's café–district frequented by Danton
3. The Bastille
4. Soldiers' home from which canons were taken for the storming of the Bastille
5. Social spot for the wealthy–shops, cafés, etc.
6. District frequented by Robespierre
7. Palace where Louis XVI and his family were held under arrest after their attempted escape
8. Sorbonne Library
9. Traditional site of executions; guillotine first used here
10. Site for the July, 1790 celebration of the fall of the Bastille
11. Neighborhood of the wealthy

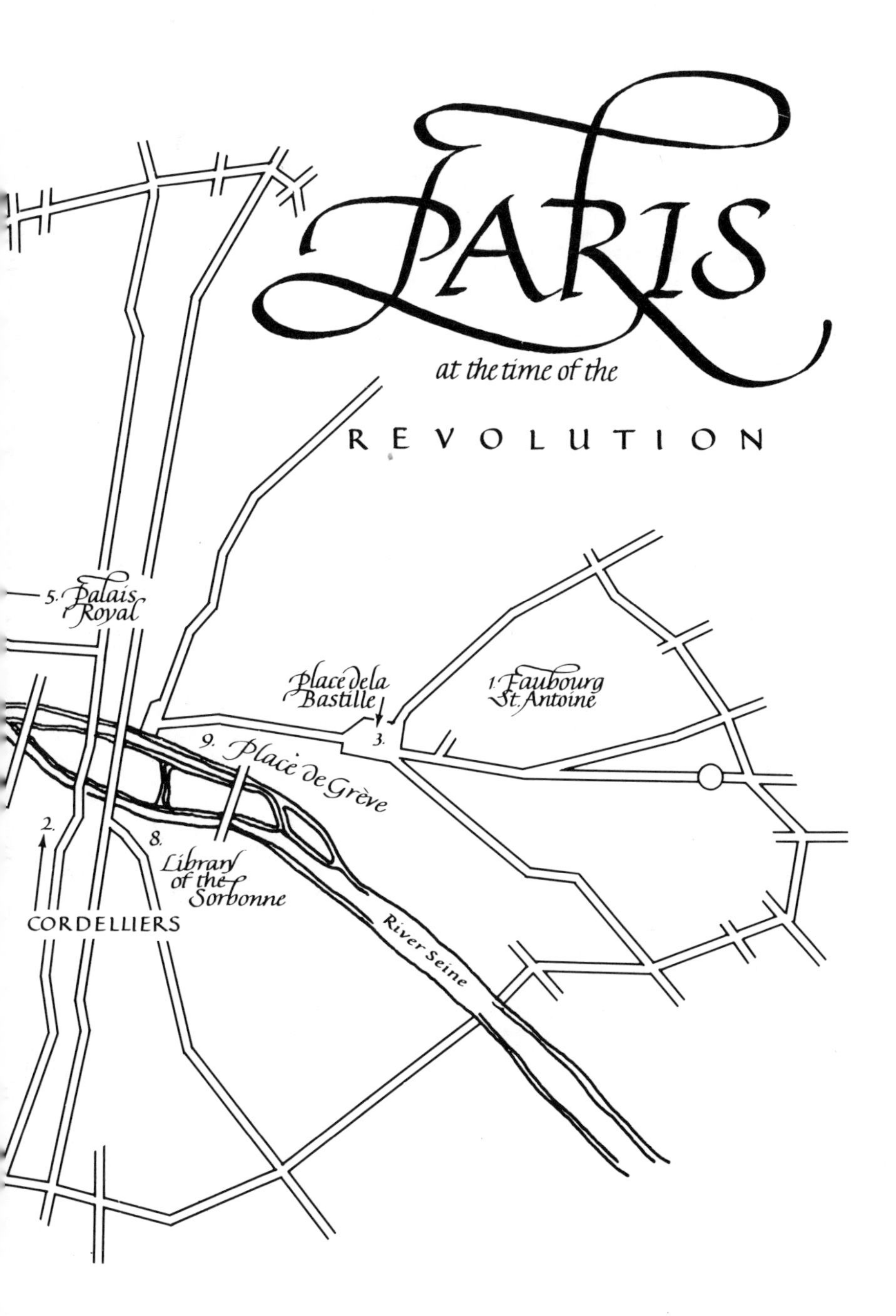
PARIS
at the time of the
REVOLUTION
5. Palais Royal
Place de la Bastille
1. Faubourg St. Antoine
3.
9. Place de Grève
2.
8.
Library of the Sorbonne
CORDELLIERS
River Seine

The fear of the Lord is the instruction of wisdom;
and before honor is humility.
Proverbs 15:13

ROLOGUE

Autumn, 1793

Keep your heart with all diligence, for out of it spring the issues of life. Proverbs 4:23

I have never been inclined to talk much about myself or my affairs. There are two reasons to account for this, I suppose. The first is simply that talk of others has always seemed more interesting to me than talk of myself. The second is that I was given by my Creator (whether as a thorn or a gift, I'm yet unsure) a reticent nature. It may seem odd, therefore, that someone of my temperament should be suddenly struck with what might be called an ''autobiographical impulse.'' But to be honest, I confess that even now as I begin to write, my inclination is the same as it has always been–to say nothing. My conscience, however, will not allow it.

As may be guessed, much of what I must write is not flattering. I can only hope that those who read this narrative will believe me when I say that by the grace of God I am not as I once was. Such hope will seem less presumptuous if, from the outset, I make clear my determination to return to France and do what I can to set things right. I am resolved to do so even if it costs me my life, as well it might, for I've been warned that the Revolution has not ended–that the sharp blade of the guillotine is yet wet with the blood of the innocent.

Though I have little way of knowing exactly *what* I shall find when I return to Paris, I know *whom* I must find. His name is Phillipe Grammônd. Though he is several years younger than I, Phillipe was once my most loyal friend. He admired me at a time when I was unworthy of admiration and loved me with a faithfulness I did not deserve. It is for him especially that I've decided to write down these thoughts and take them with me. I hope that they will help him, and others like him, to understand the mercy of the God I've come to know and love.

I write for one other friend as well, a much older and wiser friend named Pierre-Joseph Aumônt. It was he who first shared with me the Scripture, that Word which has since given me the will to live and the courage to die. It was also he who made possible my safe flight from France to England.

My escape took place about a year ago in the autumn of 1792. Louis XVI had but recently been overthrown, and with the monarchy's demise, radicals in France increased their power until the tenuous rule of law and order gave way to a reign of terror. Up to that time, I had imagined myself incapable of cowardice or cruelty. I was wrong.

In my months away from home, I've come to understand many things, not the least of which is a truth that Pierre-Joseph tried with astonishing patience to pound into my head. "You must understand, Jacques," he said repeatedly. "It is your heart–not your circumstances–that will determine whether you become a man of honor or disgrace." I was fifteen and a prisoner in the Bastille when he first spoke those words to me. Of course, I did not believe him then. But I run ahead of myself. Let me begin my story by telling you of Paris and of my place in it on the eve of the Revolution.

PART ONE
The Road to the Bastille
1787-1788

CHAPTER 1

Spring, 1787

The revolution began for me the day my father was murdered. Though it was years ago, memories of that day have faded little. His death is still difficult to think upon and harder yet to write about, and I would not, were it not for the fact that the circumstances of his death reveal the temper of the times.

It was early one afternoon. My father and I were in our shop as usual. I was bent over the fire, stirring up a new batch of molding wax while he was busy carving on yet another marble bust of the great Rousseau. He had done many such busts that spring, for Rousseau, like Voltaire, had become an idol of the rich. Requests for his image seemed endless and were not limited to sculptured busts. The wealthy wanted the face of this dead philosopher on buttons, snuff boxes, shaving bowls, and inkwells. Indeed, for several months it seemed that everywhere I looked, a Rousseau was staring back at me.

There was one thing, however, that intrigued me about those myriad faces that my father created: no two were alike. I have since come to realize that such diversity is the mark of a great artist. My father was a great artist, and I freely admit that any success I have achieved as a sculptor I owe to him. For it was he who first stood me on a stool before a block of stone, placed a chisel in my hand, and clasping his strong hand over mine, steadied the tool and laid the hammer to it. I was no more than three, but I still vividly remember the first time my hand felt iron meeting stone. From that day I was always at my father's side working with him in the shop.

I can still see him as he was that afternoon, poised on the edge of his stool, hovering over a low wooden worktable, the dust of chiseled stone clinging to his beard. I remember, too, how his face brightened the moment he laid his tools aside and bade me do the same.

''Jacques, tomorrow is your mother's birthday,'' he reminded me. ''What shall we get for her?''

His look told me that he had no need of my suggestions. Still, he had asked. So, remembering her birthdays past, I suggested some colorful linen thread for her lace work.

''No, no, Jacques,'' he said, beckoning me to bring a stool and come to sit by him. ''I want this year to be different. This year, I want to give your mother a memory–to wrap it up and place it on the table there before her.''

I was just fourteen, but at that moment something in my father's voice made me understand that he spoke to me as man to man, and though uncertain of the full meaning in his words, I sensed enough to know that I wanted to be part of his plan. I paused only a moment before asking, ''What kind of memory?''

He leaned forward, resting both hands upon his knees. ''Well,'' he continued, his voice just above a whisper, ''you know, we've never had much. Oh, my father and I had plenty of business, just as you and I do. But even good business does not provide artisans like us with the delicacies of the rich. There was one time though–just once–when your mother and I enjoyed such a delicacy. It was on our wedding day. On that day my father somehow managed to get a pigeon and prepare it for our wedding supper. Ah, Jacques,'' he sighed, ''you never tasted such a dinner.''

''However did grandfather get hold of a pigeon?'' I asked.

"I've no idea," he confessed. "But this I do know: if he did it, so can I. Your mother has often reminisced to me about that bird. And when she speaks of it, it's enough to make your mouth water. She remembers it well."

"I think it's not just the bird that she's remembering," I said.

His smile grew so broad it threatened to eclipse his face. "You're right, Jacques! Every time she thinks about that bird, she remembers that she loves me. Indeed, I think it may have been that bird that won her heart. That's why you and I are going to close up shop and pay a visit to old Michel this afternoon. He's a good man, old Michel is, and I'll wager he'll let me hunt a bird out on his land."

"Hunt?" I said. "On his small plot of land? Not much for hunting I'd say."

"Michel farms more than that one small plot. He tends the fields all around him. It's a vast acreage."

"But he does not own all the land he farms," I reminded him. "The Comte de Guiche owns most of it."

A look of anger erased the smile from my father's face. "It is Michel who keeps the land thriving, and he does so with a worn-out plow and rusty sickle. What's more, he pays good money to that fat old Comte for the 'privilege' of doing so!" He then thrust his finger in my face for emphasis. "Michel nurses the land, makes it fruitful, and pays for it. Now you tell me, who 'owns' it?"

I could not better his argument, and yet I felt I had to try. "But the laws, Papa. They say the Comte owns most of the land and *all* of the game on it–even the game on Michel's plot."

"I have come to believe, Jacques, that only a fool would say that the birds which fly over a man's field are not his!"

"Well, then," I said cautiously, "France must be full of fools."

He gazed at me a moment and then burst into a hearty laugh. "There you have it!"

My father could see that fear made it hard for me to enjoy the laughter.

"Times are changing," he assured me. "Have you not listened to the talk of those who come into the shop? They have enshrined the ideas of Rousseau as surely as they have his face. Mark me, before long they will consider it fashionable to cast aside such laws."

"Still," I argued, "the laws aren't cast aside just yet. And we don't know if the Comte de Guiche is one who's heard of such ideas."

"Every beggar in the streets of Paris has heard of such ideas!" he chided. "Come, it is *one* bird to make your mother happy. My father succeeded in bagging one, and in his day the laws were even harsher. Besides, if you are right in saying that the Comte has managed to remain ignorant of Rousseau, then it should be easy to hide my hunt from him as well."

"We'd best be going then," I said, his confidence having won me over, "or the setting sun, not the Comte de Guiche, will keep us from that bird."

"Let's to it," he said, and we got up to go. It was then we heard my mother coming down the stairs that led up to our living quarters. "Jacques," she said, quickly entering the shop and handing me one of her neatly wrapped bundles, "I need for you to deliver this lace to–"

My father intercepted the bundle and gave it back to her. "Oh no," he said. "Jacques is coming with me."

My mother stared up at him in vague surprise. "And where in the world would you be going in the middle of the day?"

"None of your business," said my father merrily. And taking off his apron, he tossed it to her.

Caught up in my father's high spirits, I too whipped off my apron and tossed it to my mother. Then, fearing she might take this bravado somewhat amiss, I added, "We won't be long, and you'll be pleased with what we bring back for you."

As we headed toward the door my mother called out after us, "Go ahead you two, go off without a word. But I warn you, I'll not keep your dinner warm if you are late." I looked back just long enough to see that her scolding was all bluff.

* * *

My anxiety returned when we reached Michel's, for I could see my former apprehension mirrored in his weathered face. ''I don't know–'' he said. ''The Comte, he's uncommon stingy with his birds.''

''You know, Michel, I'd not ask you to answer for my actions,'' said my father carefully. ''I don't want you to give me an official sanction. I just want to know–friend to friend–if it were up to you, would you mind my bagging a bird on this property?''

''If it were up to me, you know I'd bag the bird for you myself,'' he said. Then he added hotly, ''Why, I'd bag you a whole slew of 'em. Those flying thieves raid my seed at every harvest, then fly home to the safety of the Comte's dovecote!'' He paused and grew cautious once again. ''What's mine I'd just as soon be yours. I can loan you a gun, but–''

My father stopped him. ''That's all I ask, the loan of a gun and your word that whatever else you could give, you would give.'' With that assurance, old Michel handed my father his gun, doffed his ragged cap, and left us.

It was late afternoon by the time we finally set out, and another quarter of an hour passed before we came to an open stretch of land. ''I'll wager,'' said my father, pointing out a brushy area in the distance, ''I can flush a nice fat bird out of that brush over there.''

''What can I do to help?'' I asked.

''Wait here,'' he said, the excitement growing in his voice. ''Two of us would make too much noise. You can keep a lookout for me.''

I watched his lean, agile form set out across the field and thought proudly that he was yet a good man to have in any fight. The quiet beauty of the open land calmed my fears and restored my faith in him, and as I sat down under an old gnarled tree to wait, I no longer doubted that he would bag that bird.

It was not long before a shot rang out. Jumping to my feet, I saw my father emerging from the brush, holding up his treasure for me to see. I was about to shout my congratulations, but before I could give voice to it, I spied a young man decked out in finery riding fast toward my father from the east. He too must have heard the shot. I tried to cry a warning, but the words stuck in my throat like some suffocating thing. Nor did I move. I simply watched the man as he came on, his fine muscular horse silhouetted against the burning brightness of the setting sun, its graceful form hardly touching hoof to ground.

He reached my father and reigned in, but did not dismount. They spoke, and from where I stood, I saw neither fear nor shame upon my father's face during the course of this short exchange. Then I remember my father holding up that bird. I expected the young nobleman simply to reach down and take it. Instead he pulled a pistol from his riding boot, shot my father in the chest, and rode off as if he'd killed a rabbit.

I found my voice and took off at a run, crying out my father's name as I fled to him across the field. To this day I do not know if anyone heard my screaming. I know that I did not care. At that moment I cared for one thing only–the sound of my father's voice answering mine.

When I reached him, he lay sprawled on his back, his hand still clutching fast the lifeless bird. The blood was flowing freely from his heart, and I knew before I kneeled to touch him–he was dead. He looked so strange lying there amidst the new grown grass and wildflowers. How I wished that the same April sun that had but recently touched dry roots long sleeping, bringing them to life, could have touched my father also and awakened him again. The world changed for me that moment as I knelt beside my father, lifeless in the field.

* * *

My mother and I survived those days immediately following my father's death by keeping alive our hope that his murderer, whom we learned was the older of the Comte de Guiche's two sons, would be brought to justice. By summer's end, "justice" had been meted out. The Comte's wealth and influence insured that the court would be lenient; the young nobleman was sentenced only "to pay a fee to the widow and orphan of the dead man."

I well remember the rage on my mother's face when that young man, only a few years older than I, stepped forward and handed her his bulging bag of coins. I think he actually believed that she would take it, for he seemed genuinely astonished when she emptied its contents into her hand and threw it at his feet. He was doubly astonished when she spit in his face before turning on her heel and exiting the courtroom.

By the time we reached the shop, her rage had given way to grief. She wept almost unceasingly for several days. Then she stopped her weeping. Burying her hopes with my father, she gave way to complete despair.

HAPTER 2

Spring, 1788

Unlike my mother, I did not despair after my father's death. Nor did I vent my rage in public as she had done that day in the courtroom. Indeed, it would have been impossible for me to rid myself of such anger in a moment of passion. No, my rage went too deep, and deeply did I harbor it until it became so much a part of me that I ceased to see it for what it was. I believed my growing sullenness to be the outworking of genuine sorrow and my increasing peevishness the legitimate reflection of a creative nature.

If there was any advantage to this melancholy brought on by anger, it was that it drove me to my work. I felt at peace only when I was busy in my shop. The sturdy feel of my hammer and chisel coupled with the measured sound of iron striking stone seemed somehow to quiet my feverish spirit. Such discipline hastened the establishment of my reputation. Within a year I was looked upon as a master artisan whose work could evoke a nod of approval from the most obstinate nobleman.

Still, the fact that I could satisfy wealthy customers did not insure that my mother and I would be well fed. There were several reasons for this, one of which affected all of us who labored in

St. Antoine. The year's harvest had been meager and the winter harsh. Food and firewood were scarce even for those who could afford them. Beggars in the streets of Paris had increased twofold, and I began to fear that my mother and I might soon be forced to join them. But during this unhappy time there was one bit of light I allowed into my otherwise dismal existence. It was Phillipe, the eight-year-old son of the cabinetmaker, Thomas Grammônd, whose shop was also on our street.

Shortly after my father's death, Phillipe began his daily visits to my shop. He had wandered in one day and had become as intrigued with my work as I had been with my father's. I suppose that was what first endeared him to me–that and his boundless energy and unfailing good nature, both of which did much to lift my spirits as I worked. I remember one day in particular.

I had just completed a bust commissioned by a squire named Latude when Phillipe came bursting in and announced quite unnecessarily, "I'm here!" In a moment his cap and jacket were tossed into the corner, and he was dragging a stool over to my worktable. "It's Monsieur Latude," he said, as he climbed up on the stool.

"And how do you know the 'good' monsieur?" I asked, gratified that I had apparently achieved a good likeness of the squire.

"He's been coming into Papa's shop for weeks," Phillipe informed me. "He has ordered a cabinet, but he's hard to please. Each time Papa thinks he's finished carving, Monsieur Latude demands another leaf or flower. You should hear Papa after he has gone. It's enough to scorch your ears!"

The news was not encouraging. "Perhaps he will like his face better than he likes his cabinet." I said.

It was then that I noticed Phillipe's expression. Something about the bust was bothering him. Though he was only eight, I had come to realize that Phillipe had a keen eye, and his appraisals, if nothing else, were always honest–sometimes brutally so. I braced myself. "What's the matter?" I asked. "Don't you like it?"

"Oh, it isn't that," he assured me.

``Well, what is it then?''

I can still see him as he leaned both elbows on the worktable and peered closely at the face. His unruly auburn hair fell down across his forehead and his blue-black eyes were fixed in concentration on my work.

``Well?'' I prodded.

``His nose,'' said Phillipe. ``It is the nose.''

``What about the nose?''

``It's not big enough,'' he concluded. Then, with the confident air of a critic, he leaned back, folded his arms across his chest, and said yet more emphatically. ``Monsieur Latude's nose is much bigger.''

``But Monsieur Latude does not believe that,'' I explained.

Phillipe was yet too young–and honest–to enjoy the art of vain deceit. ``How can he not believe it?'' he demanded. ``It is on *his* face.''

``That is precisely why he does not,'' I said. Phillipe's trust in me began to erode his confidence, and I remember that he lifted his hand and rubbed his own nose as if to make certain that he knew its size.

``One day you'll understand,'' I assured him. ``For now you must trust that I have made Monsieur Latude's nose exactly as he wants it.'' Of course, I did not admit to him the pleasure that it gave me to play upon the vanity of such men; it was a form of scorn.

``Speaking of what Monsieur Latude wants,'' I continued, ``he has asked me to deliver this to Charpentier's café. Monsieur Charpentier has promised me that he will deliver the bust *and* see that I am paid.'' For several months I'd been seeking out commissions at Charpentier's to supplement those that came directly to the shop.

``Do you want me to stay and listen for the shop bell until your mother returns?'' he asked.

``She's here–'' I admitted; then I hesitated. ``But she is upstairs–sleeping.''

"She is always sleeping these days," he observed.

I ignored his comment and said instead, "If you will stay and listen for the bell, I will give you some molding wax to work with."

"And a story when you return?"

I nodded my consent.

"I will stay as long as you like," he promised.

"Good," I said, scooping some wax onto a pan and placing it in front of him. "I will be gone the remainder of the afternoon and perhaps on into early evening."

Carefully I wrapped a cloth about the bust of Latude. "Just get the name and address from any customers that come for me," I continued.

"If someone comes wanting to buy your mama's lace, do you want me to go upstairs and wake her?"

"No–" I said a bit too harshly.

Phillipe looked up. "Shall I tell them to come tomorrow then?"

"No," I said and tried to search for some excuse that would make him cease his questioning. "Just tell them that she is ill and that I–I'm not sure when she will be feeling better." As an afterthought I added, "Of course, they can leave their name if they would like."

Despite my efforts, Phillipe sensed my growing irritation, and although he had no idea why I had turned peevish, he tried in his childlike way to make things better, saying, "It's all right. I don't think that anyone will come. The bell does not ring much for her anymore."

I got up quickly, picked up the bust, and headed out. At the door I turned to see him staring after me. "You need not stay inside the whole time," I said, trying to sound more cheerful. "Go outside a little; you can easily see any customers approaching in this alley. Oh, and if you get hungry before I return, there's some fruit over on the table in the corner."

He smiled and waved before plunging both hands into the molding wax. I went out, closing the door behind me. As I did so, the soft tinkling of the shop bell reminded me of Phillipe's innocent observation, ''The bell does not ring much for her anymore.''

CHAPTER 3

I had hoped that the atmosphere at Charpentier's would lift my spirits. It often did, but this day when I entered, I sensed a subtle, unsettled feeling, as if something unusual or unpleasant were about to happen. Moving toward my usual corner, I studied the customers as I went. They seemed the usual clientele: lawyers in court robes languidly sipping cider and talking politics; town clerks and country squires gaming and grumbling at crowded tables. Everything seemed as always–the lawyers, the clerks, the low hum of conversation punctuated by the soft tapping of dominos and drinking mugs on marbled tabletops.

Within moments Charpentier approached and diverted my attention with his usual friendly goading. "So you are here again."

"Yes, I'm here again," I said, somewhat heartened by his greeting. "And I'll be here again tomorrow. Come, admit it, you would miss me if I stayed away."

"It's true," he said laughing. Then growing serious he added, "Still, Jacques, you might take an afternoon off now and then; you never seem to relax, to enjoy yourself."

"That's why I come here," I said. "The games and conversation are relaxing."

"And, of course, every *sou* is important."

"I do well enough," I said defensively; then catching myself, I softened my tone. "My mother's lacemaking is the pride of Paris. She does a good business. Along with what I make, we are doing better than most. But–you are right, I do enjoy earning a few extra *sous*–just for myself."

"As you should enjoy making an honest wage for honest work," he said, his jovial spirit restored. "I see you have brought Latude," he added.

I unwrapped the bust and handed it to him. It was about twelve inches in height but when Charpentier took it in his massive hands, it seemed almost to disappear.

"I will say this for you, Jacques," he said, a faint smile playing at the corners of his mouth. "Though you are sometimes gloomy, you are certainly gifted. I do not understand how you can make a block of marble look as supple and smooth as muscle and bone."

"My father would have told you that what you hold in your hand was never simply stone," I said, warming to the subject of my art. "He taught me that in every block of marble there is a living face or figure waiting to be freed; the sculptor's job is simply to release the captive from the unchiseled stone that binds him."

Charpentier knew well that the memory of my father might draw me deeper into melancholy, and he did his best to avert the possibility. "Well, I must say that you've let Latude escape. But I warn you, there may be some who will not thank you that he's freed."

"It's too late now," I said.

Setting the bust aside, he continued, "It won't be long before all of my customers will be begging for a bust of themselves. You have come to the right place, Jacques, for I tell you that wherever there are lawyers, a sculptor need not want for work.

Such men love busts of themselves. They set them on their mantels next to their collection of Rousseaus and Voltaires. Ah yes," he sighed, "such men pride themselves on their image." Then leaning close, he added, "Though just between you and me, as I look at them I cannot see why."

I smiled, and seeing his success, he added, "Then again, next to the pinched and sallow face of old Voltaire, would not even I look handsome?"

"Indeed," I assured him, laughing outright.

"Poor old Voltaire. Had he lived another ten years, I am certain that he would have begged you to do a bust of him." Charpentier paused a moment to cast another glance at the face of Latude before adding, "I have noted that you rarely fail to make your subjects look a bit better than they really are. Eh?"

"Perhaps," I confessed.

"I knew it!" he said. "You are more than a good sculptor; you are a clever businessman. And I predict that both will pay you well one day."

"I hope that you are right."

"Charpentier is *always* right," he said. "Trust me, you will one day be the talk of Paris. You will not forget me?"

"Of course not," I said.

"Good. Now go settle yourself and I will bring you some cider."

Taking Charpentier's advice, I moved over to the staircase and leaned against one of the wooden beams to wait for the casual nod of a customer to summon me. As I waited, a vague sense of guilt came over me, for I knew that I had not been honest with Charpentier. I did need money–desperately–and not just because of a meager harvest and harsh winter. My mother and I together should have been able to survive better than most. Indeed, her lacemaking had been the pride of Paris, but not of late–not since the Comte de Guiche's son had murdered my father.

I had lied to Phillipe as well. My mother had been sleeping, but her sleep was more than that brought on by ill health; it was the sleep of drunkenness. The deft hands that once wove delicate patterns now did little more than clutch a flask of sour wine. For months I had made excuses to her customers, but I rarely had to do so anymore. Her commissions had dropped off drastically, and what little money she did make, she hoarded to buy more wine. She drank and slept only to awake and drink some more. The only people I lied to now were friends.

I closed my eyes, determined to push down unwanted thoughts and feelings. Then, as if in answer to the tension that had gripped me, a booming voice called out, "Citizens!" I snapped to attention, as did every other man in the café. It was not unusual for a customer to demand attention. But as this man emerged from a darkened corner of the room, I could see that he was no usual customer.

He was a giant of a man, and although he was fashionably dressed, fashion ill-suited him. The gray breeches and white stockings that he wore clung to his muscular legs and thighs as if every thread were strained; his red-striped waistcoat bulged at every button; and the lace-trimmed cravat looked ludicrous around his bull-like neck. As for his face–I had never seen such a profoundly ugly face. His skin was marred and pitted by the ravages of smallpox, and his large square jaw was rounded out by massive sagging jowls. There was a scar that split his upper lip, and the dark eyes receded beneath wild, bushy eyebrows.

Not a sound could be heard as this stranger moved to the center of the room, and with cool impudence stated flatly, "I need money."

The customers were dumbfounded, unable to decide whether this powerful man were a great orator or a mere mountebank. He did not wait for their decision.

"I see you blush that I so boldly confess to you my plight. But why? Does not the King himself admit as much?" He pulled a tattered news sheet from his waistcoat and held it up. "We are told here that France is poor, that His Majesty is poor, and that we the people must be taxed to pay his debts. But I, Georges Danton, cannot pay his debts. Can you? Or you? Are we not mere clerks and counselors? We know that the wealthy nobles will not pay. Then I ask you again, who shall pay? The peasants who strain to wrench the rye and buckwheat from the soil?''

As Danton began to move among the crowd, I noted what to my artist's eye was an amazing transformation. This strange man's eloquence not only swayed his hearers but changed his face as well. The dark eyes sparkled brightly, and every facial muscle sprang to life. Such animation transformed this grotesque giant of a man into a mighty warrior.

''Where has the wealth of our great nation gone?'' he bellowed. ''We were not always poor. I tell you it has gone to support the profligate living of that Austrian woman, Marie-Antoinette, whom His Majesty calls our queen. She is not *our* queen, and we will not pay her debts! We cannot! And though we love our king, we will not allow his wife to drive us into bankruptcy!''

A round of applause rang out. I could see that without doubt Danton had his audience now, and with the skill of a Roman orator he continued the harangue, a harangue I felt sure would go on for hours. Such speakers were seldom brief once they succeeded in arresting the attention of Charpentier's clientele. My spirits sank. I realized that there would be no hope of new commissions this day. Nor could I expect Charpentier to interrupt this exchange between a café orator and his audience to wrench payment from Latude. What did such men know of poverty, men in velvet robes, silk waistcoats, and buckled shoes? To them all this was no more than rhetoric–not to me. Slowly I made my way along the wall, determined to slip out.

CHAPTER 4

As I stepped out into the street, the bells atop one of the cathedrals began to ring. The music of those bells was like laughter in that part of the city where the gaily dressed promenaded along the Rue St. Honoré and gossiped in shops lining the Palais-Royal. But well I knew that when the soft winds on the river Seine picked up this music and carried it away from the city's heart, its fading echoes would fall on the ear like weeping and, at length, die out as a sigh.

I looked across to the cobbled wharf that ran along the Seine. The amber hues of a dying sun made the gray stones seem warm, inviting. As I turned toward home, I crossed the street that I might walk along the water.

The cool, damp mist felt good upon my face, and as I walked, my thoughts were drawn more and more to the river, that river which for hundreds of years had pumped life into a thriving city. It seemed at that moment to be pumping life back into me as well, life that weeks and months of strain had sucked out of me. Undisturbed, the river flowed past palaces and prisons with the same ever-constant rhythm. An overwhelming desire rose in my heart, a desire to capture the secret of such constancy. Why, I wondered, can I not move through life like the river Seine, oblivious to pain–or even pleasure?

By the time I reached St. Antoine it was growing dark. I rounded the corner to my shop, still lost in thought, but was quickly jerked from my reverie when through the dusk I saw the chalk-white face of Phillipe. He stood pressed against my shop door, clutching in his hands a bunch of grapes. A wild pig had cornered him and with a menacing look was eyeing the fruit that Phillipe grasped tightly in his hand.

Grabbing up a loosened stone, I flew down the alley, crying as I ran, "Throw the fruit, Phillipe! Throw it!" But Phillipe was too frightened to obey. Seeing that the animal was about to lunge, I skidded to a stop and hurled the rock. With a vicious squeal the lean, rangy thing turned. I had no time to find another stone. The animal was racing toward me. I threw my back against the alley wall and braced myself. When the beast attacked, I kicked at it with all my strength. A shooting pain went up my leg as its razor sharp teeth sliced across my ankle, but my kick had been sure enough to daze the animal. The pain that the animal inflicted unleashed in me all the pent-up rage of a long, frustrating day, and with renewed strength I jumped over the beast, sweeping up another stone as I landed on its other side. Screaming, I lunged and threw again. It was enough; the animal took off squealing down the alley.

"Little wonder that there are no promenaders outside our shops!" I yelled at no one in particular. "It's not even safe for beggars where wild pigs run free!"

Then, remembering Phillipe, I turned to see him still standing, rooted to the spot. My blood was still up as I rushed to him. "How many times must I tell you, Phillipe?" I took him by the shoulders. "Never, never eat in the alley! You are sure to lose an arm–or worse."

He lifted a trembling hand and offered up his fruit. The slender fingers which held the grapes–quite crushed by now–reminded me of the talons of a tiny bird. My anger melted. "Go ahead and eat what's left of them,'' I said, slumping down to take a seat on the narrow steps. ''It's safe now.''

Phillipe sat down beside me. ''Your leg–it's bleeding.''

''It will stop in a moment,'' I said. ''He didn't get his teeth into me. I was too fast for him.''

''You *were* fast,'' he said, an admiring smile lighting up his face. As he shoved the dripping grapes into his mouth, he asked, ''Do I still get a story?''

I marveled at how quickly he had shed his fear. ''How about a story of a wild pig?'' I said.

He gave me a look of scorn. ''That wouldn't be a story,'' he said. ''That's real.''

''Real things *do* happen in stories,'' I reminded him.

He thought on that for a moment, then resolutely began, ''That's not the kind of story I want. I want–'' He stopped. ''Who's that?''

I followed Phillipe's gaze down the alley to see a stranger moving slowly toward us, stopping long enough to briefly examine the shop signs as he passed. Despite the dusky shadows that clouded the features of his face, I soon recognized the man.

''I don't like the look of him,'' said Phillipe. ''What do you think he wants?''

''We need not wait and see,'' I said, feeling no inclination to admit that I knew who he was. ''Let's go inside.''

As I reached for the shop door, I heard again that booming voice ring out. ''There you are!''

Reluctantly I turned. Danton was fast approaching.

''I saw you slip out as I began my speech,'' he said, when at length he stood before us. ''Oh, I don't blame you,'' he continued, ignoring the cool reception I was giving him. ''I didn't care much for politics at your age either.''

Danton reached down and placed one hand upon Phillipe. ''I remember what I liked and did not like at your age too. Back then I was quite a scrapper. As a matter of fact, I was just about your age when I got this scar,'' he said, pointing proudly to his mouth. "I had a fight with a bull. It was his horn that split my lip. I didn't let him get away with it, though. Three days later, I was out in the pasture again with a stick and gave him as good a beating as he had given me. Of course, he also broke my nose that time. Still I felt I'd settled matters." He sighed contentedly before adding, "Yes, back then I was quite a scrapper."

"I'm not a scrapper," said Phillipe, pulling back.

It was obvious that he liked Danton no more than I did. Still, I'd had enough for one night, and wanting to make certain that there would be no confrontation, I said, "You'd better be getting home, Phillipe. I'll see you tomorrow."

Phillipe did not seem loath to go. He lingered only a moment at his father's shop door. "Thanks, Jacques," he said, calling back to me. "You *were* fast."

Before Danton could inquire as to the cause of Phillipe's admiration, I turned to him and quickly asked, "What is it that you want?"

"Charpentier showed me the bust you brought to him and assured me that you are as skilled in sculpting wax as you are in chiseling stone." He paused only for a moment to see how I registered such praise. I did my best to keep my face impassive, and after a moment he continued. "He warned me, too, that you were a no-nonsense sort, so I will come quickly to my point. I have a commission for you."

I wanted to refuse outright, but my need of money forced me to hold my tongue.

"I'd like a portrait medallion of myself," he continued. Then leaning closer, he added with a smile, "It's for a lady."

The feeling of Danton's hot breath upon my face was loathsome, and instinctively I backed away. "It can be done," I said.

He did not seem to notice my aversion. "Good! It need not be large. A miniature will do, one that she can carry in her hand. You understand?"

I nodded. "I have done such miniatures before."

"How long before it's done?" he asked.

I hesitated only a moment before saying, ''I shall have it for you the day after tomorrow.''

''Splendid!'' he cried.

I knew that I would have to work day and night to meet such a deadline, but wanting to be done with this man soon as possible, I determined to do so.

''Shall I come in now and let you get a sketch of me then?'' he asked.

''That's not necessary. I've a good memory for faces.''

''Especially for ones like mine?'' he asked, carefully gauging my expression. I said nothing, and just as the silence was becoming oppressive, he burst into a roar of laughter. ''Day after tomorrow then!'' he said. Turning on his heel, he headed down the alley, laughing as he went; the very walls shook with it, but somehow the sound was hollow, a laughter without merriment.

CHAPTER 5

I crushed the sculpted face beneath my fist, got up, and paced about the room. For the first time in my life, my artistry had utterly failed me. I had tried all day, through the night, and into the morning. But try as I would, the wax refused to yield to me. I cursed my own stupidity. This time I had expected too much of myself. Danton's was not a face for portraits. But how was I to explain that to him?

Wearily I returned to my worktable and gazed down upon the medallion once more. The pressure of my blow had twisted Danton's mouth into a macabre grin. Oddly enough, the damage seemed almost unnoticeable beneath the strong forehead and penetrating eyes. Perhaps, I thought, I've gone about it wrongly. I've been trying to obscure his ugliness, but there is no obscuring it.

I thought back to the café and to the strange transformation that came over him as he warmed to his speech. I remembered that fine line between the ugliness of his features and their strength. That's it, I thought. I must see him as he was that evening. I set to work again, this time determined to fix my mind on that moment when one saw Danton not as hideous but as Herculean.

I was well on my way to restoring the mouth when my concentration was broken by a stirring upstairs. My mother had awakened. Quickly I took the two wine bottles I had taken from her room the night before and put them out of sight with others I'd retrieved. I wanted desperately to stay at my work, but I knew that she needed to eat and would not unless I forced her to it. Reluctantly, I pulled myself away and went upstairs.

She gave me a half-hearted smile as she slowly shuffled across the room to sit down at the kitchen table. My heart sank as I watched her. She was terribly thin and sallow-looking. Her long hair, which she–and my father–had been so proud of, now hung limp about her face, void of any sheen. So too, her eyes that once reflected all the vibrant greens of summer were now dull, lifeless.

As she sat down at the kitchen table, I saw her glance about, searching for the wine.

"Let me fix you some bread and cheese," I said quickly.

"I'm not hungry," she replied in a voice that was barely audible.

"You must eat. You're wasting away," I said, hurrying to prepare her meal. "You refused me all day yesterday, but I'm telling you that you *will* eat today."

She took no notice of either my firmness or my frantic preparations. Her concentration remained fixed on searching out the room, even when I placed her meal before her.

"Where is it?" she said as she pushed the plate aside.

"I have put it away," I said resolutely, but I could not bring myself to look at her.

Gathering her strength, she raised herself to face me. "Who are you to tell your mother when she must eat and when she must not drink?"

I forced myself to look her in the face. "I am your son and I refuse to let you starve!"

For a moment her green eyes flashed with their former beauty as she raised her hand to strike me. I caught her by the wrist before the blow could fall. I felt her frailness, and she my strength. The fury in her seemed to melt. "Please, Jacques, you do not understand." Her pleading was more painful than any blow she could have given me.

I stood there fighting with myself, trying to steel my heart against the look in her eyes. But I could not. "I will give you more wine," I said, "after you have eaten."

She collapsed into the chair, pulled the food towards herself, and forced herself to eat.

I hated myself for giving in, but I could not fight her. But neither could I ease her pain. I could only keep her alive, and I *would* keep her alive. Yet as I looked at her sitting there, I felt that the mother I had known was already dead. This woman that sat before me was no more than her shadow. Still, I could not help but love even the shadow of her.

"I've eaten it all," she said looking up at me.

Reluctantly I went down into the shop, retrieved the wine, and brought it to her.

She took it from me and got up. Pausing a moment, she placed her hand on my shoulder, "Thank you, son," she said. Then once again she disappeared behind the curtain where she slept.

I salved my conscience by telling myself that all she needed was a bit more time. I could give her that–time and patience. I determined more than ever to protect her (and myself) from those who would be quick to condemn. No one need know that my mother's heart, mind, and hands had all failed her.

I was still standing there, looking after her, when I heard the shop bell ring. I went downstairs to see Danton waiting for me.

"Good morning," he said cheerfully.

"Good morning," I returned without the cheer.

"Come," said Danton, "is working on my portrait that depressing?"

I drew my thoughts back to the business at hand. "I regret to say that I was unable to finish the medallion you requested."

"Was it the deadline or the subject that hindered you?"

I paused a moment. ''To be honest, it was both. But I believe I could have mastered the subject if I had had the time.''

''Take all the time you need,'' he said.

His response caught me off guard, for I fully expected him to turn on his heel and leave. Any of my other customers would have done so.

''I see you are unaccustomed to patience,'' he said wryly. ''But I would wager that I am not like most of your other customers. They may not understand the value of hard labor, but I do. I have worked hard, and only recently has my work come to pay me well.''

He stopped a moment and glanced about the shop. Then, reaching into his pocket, he pulled out some money–enough to pay for at least half of the commission–and held it out to me.

I forced myself to say, ''You need not pay until I've finished.''

''Take it,'' he urged. ''I know you will finish as quickly as you can. And I have no doubt that I will be pleased with the work, for I know that you will not present it to me until you are well pleased with it yourself.''

I took the money and casually laid it on my worktable, as if I was accustomed to having it about. ''I will finish your commission as soon as possible,'' I promised.

''Take it to Charpentier's when you are done,'' he said. ''I will see you there.'' He bowed politely and went out. I stood a moment, wondering if perhaps I had misjudged the man. At the time, I did not realize that for men like Danton, an act of kindness is merely a means of manipulation.

HAPTER 6

Danton had scarcely left the shop before Phillipe came bursting in, his cap askew and his rumpled jacket obviously put on in haste. ''Hurry, Jacques!'' he shouted. ''You must come quickly!''

''Come where? What are you talking about?'' I asked, trying to get him to stand still long enough for me to make some sense of his errand.

''It's Papa. He's gone after Latude!'' he said, growing even more frantic.

''What for?''

''The cabinet he's been working on for weeks–Latude sent word–he's changed his mind. He doesn't want it.''

''He can't do that.''

''Well, he has!'' Phillipe assured me. ''And now Papa's gone after him, saying he will get his due one way or another. Mama says that we must stop him!''

''All right, calm down. Just tell me which way he went. I've no idea where Latude lives.''

''Just outside the city gate,'' Phillipe said, as he turned to race for the door. ''I've got the address.''

"Wait," I said catching hold of him. "Give it to me."

He obeyed. "All right, but I'm coming too," he added.

"No, you're not," I said as I threw aside my apron. "Go home and take care of your mother."

"I must come, Jacques," he pleaded.

"No," I said more sternly. "You'll only slow me down." The point hit home, and reluctantly he headed toward the door.

Grabbing up my jacket, I ran out behind him, locking the door behind me.

"I promise that I will bring your father home safely," I called back to him; then I flew down the alleyway, glancing at the address long enough to be certain which direction I should run.

I counted on the fact that Phillipe's father, Thomas, would take the most direct, albeit crowded, route to the outskirts of the city. My instinct was correct, and within minutes I saw him up ahead of me. He was walking swiftly through the crowd, seemingly oblivious to the jostling he was giving several passers-by, and I could see that more than one of them turned on him angrily. He ignored them.

When I got closer, I shouted, "Thomas!" I was sure that he could hear my shouting; still, he didn't stop. So I kept on running, dodging people with greater care than he did.

"Thomas!" I called again when I was just about upon him.

He did not turn, but merely said, "I've got important business, Jacques. Go home."

"I know your business," I said, falling into step beside him, "and I'm not turning back. I've just left Phillipe with the promise that I would bring you home."

He stopped dead in the middle of the street, stared me in the face, and in a voice with an edge as hard as steel he said, "I, too, have made promises to Phillipe–promises to feed and clothe him. If you have found out where I'm going, then you know why I'm going. Don't try to stop me."

"I've no intention of trying to stop you," I told him flatly.

My answer was not what he expected. Indeed, it was not what I had planned to say, but it was out now. The look in his eye and the edge in his voice had awakened my own feelings of injustice. I saw myself as I had been more than a year before, standing in a courtroom expectantly waiting for some "justice" to be served upon the Comte de Guiche's son. The memory of it sickened me. "I–I will help you," I said.

He stood trying to reconcile my words with his first impressions of my mission.

"Do you have a plan? " I pressed him.

For the first time I saw him waver in his determination. "I will decide what to do when I get there," he said.

"Look, even if you can come up with a plan," I reasoned, "I doubt that you can accomplish it alone." He was listening intently to me now. "I think I know how you can get the money that is due you. Or is it revenge you're after?"

"I'd like revenge," he said honestly, "but I will settle for the money."

"Then I think we can succeed."

"You seem very sure of yourself," he said.

"Not of myself, but of Latude," I answered. "I know that he goes to Charpentier's every afternoon. If you can wait for a couple of hours, I think we can get into his chateau–and out again–without being seen." I was growing more sure of the idea that was forming in my mind as I gave voice to it.

"I'm willing to wait," he assured me. "But it will not hurt us to do our waiting just outside his gate."

"All right," I conceded. "But promise me that you–that we–will take no more than is our due."

"I am not a thief, Jacques. I am an honest artisan who has been robbed!"

His words salved my guilty conscience for the moment, and we set out and arrived at Latude's with less than a quarter of an hour to wait.

About half past three, from our hiding place we spotted Latude climbing into his carriage.

"Come on," Thomas urged.

"Not yet," I said, panicking. "His driver will see us."

"Not if we stay low and get into those bushes lining the gate. Come. If we don't get closer, we will never get inside. We have to get through the gate when it opens for the carriage."

I knew he had a point, for the iron gate that led into Latude's estate would not be easy to scale in daylight.

We moved forward slowly. "Get down! Get down! They're coming through," I said. But the sound of horses' hooves and carriage wheels on cobblestone had already convinced Thomas to press himself into the tangled foliage.

When the carriage reached the gate, a valet jumped down from the seat next to the driver. I thought that he had seen us, but I breathed a halting sigh when I realized that he'd alighted merely to swing open the gate. He opened first the side of the gate closest to us. He then moved to the opposite side of the carriage to open the other gate as well, and moving forward, he began to guide the horses through.

"Now!" I said.

Shielded by the carriage, we scrambled inside the gate and rolled into the shrubs which stood like sentinels along the bars of iron. The pawing of the horses–the only ones to sense our movement–obscured the noise we made.

"Whoa!" cried the surprised valet, and Thomas and I did not so much as breathe. It seemed hours rather than minutes before the horses calmed, allowing the valet to close the gate and mount his carriage seat again.

"We've done it!" Thomas cried when at last the sounds of the horses and their carriage had completely died away.

"We've not succeeded yet," I said, my apprehension growing. The stupidity of our plan was finally beginning to dawn on me, but I could see that Thomas was in no mood to turn back now.

"How long does he stay at Charpentier's?" he asked.

''Well into the evening,'' I assured him.

''Good.'' He sounded relieved. ''We should be able to get what we want and hide back here until the sun goes down. We'll have to scale the fence once it is dark.'' I nodded my assent. His plan was as good as any I'd thus far conceived, for I had given no thought to the problem of getting out once we'd gotten in.

''What's next?'' he asked me.

''I think the servants' entrance would be the best place to start.''

''What if there are servants there?''

''Trust me,'' I said with a confidence I did not feel. ''Now that Latude has departed for his nightly bout at the café, the servants will have vanished.''

Cautiously we made our way across the grounds until we reached the back. ''There it is,'' I said.

''How can you be sure?''

''They all look pretty much alike,'' I said. ''I've delivered lace to many of my mother's wealthy customers. Believe me, they do not let the lacemaker's son enter the front door.''

''Well, I hope the inside is as familiar to you as the outside.''

I was hoping the same thing as we crept along the wall, endeavoring to glimpse inside each window that we passed.

When we reached the door, we found it slightly ajar. I raised my hand to gently push it open but Thomas stopped me. ''What will we do if someone's in there?''

''I–I'll just tell them that Latude has ordered some lace and that my mother misplaced his order. I've come for it again.''

''Knock, then,'' he whispered.

''Knock?'' I said, staring at him incredulously.

''Of course,'' he snapped. ''That's the only way they would believe such a story.''

I knocked gently. Thomas, seeing my timidity, stepped in front of me and rapped boldly on the door. No one stirred.

"I guess you were right," he said. "They must take off as soon as Latude heads out."

We entered cautiously and looked about. We were in the kitchen.

"Well, everything's in perfect order; they won't be coming back to tidy up," he said. "But what now? Should I look for the stairs?"

"No, over here," I said, moving across the room to stand before what looked like a large cupboard in the corner. I tried the door and it opened.

"What's that?" Thomas asked, peering over my shoulder to have a closer look.

"It's a sort of moving cupboard. They put dishes, drinks, all sorts of things into it and then pull on this rope to heave it all up to the next floor. I've seen it in other houses. A servant showed it to me once. Get in."

"Are you crazy?"

"I know it's a tight fit, but it's the safest way. I'll heave you up slowly. When you reach the top, crack open the cupboard and see if the coast is clear. If it is, get out and get your money's worth. If I'm not mistaken, you'll be in the dining room. A couple of pieces of silver should cover the cost of what he owes you. When you're back inside, tap twice and I'll haul you down."

Thomas ran his hands over every inch of the cupboard. "It's good sturdy wood," he finally said. "I guess it'll hold me."

Handing me his cap, he climbed up and wedged himself in sideways. The uncertain look upon his face as he crouched there made me think more of a frightened boy than of a thief. I imagine anyone looking on would have seen the same look on my face as well.

"Here we go," I said. "Remember, be careful but be quick. And it's two taps. I'll be waiting." I closed the cupboard door and pulled down on the rope; it took more strength than I'd imagined. My progress was slow but sure. I pulled and pulled until the rope would go no further; then I wound it round a hook on the wall to secure it, and I waited.

My nerves were as tightly wound as that cupboard rope. As I waited I heard every creak of the ancient mansion, and such sounds conjured up all sorts of images. At one moment I believed there were footsteps behind me; the next instant I was certain that I'd heard the squeaking hinges of the kitchen door. Every sound–even my own breathing–became like a roaring in my ears until even the scampering of the kitchen mice across the floor seemed loud and menacing.

At last I heard the long awaited tapping against wood. Quickly I unknotted the rope and slowly let him down–a much easier task than it had been to heave him up. As soon as the rope went slack, Thomas pushed open the door, but the smile on his face vanished. I had no time to discern the cause, for at that moment a calloused hand took me by the shoulder. I turned to see two men, each holding a kitchen knife.

"Need some help there, lad?" one servant said in a menacing tone. He turned to the other. "Go, raise the alarm." Then, turning back to us, he said, "I hope you two enjoy the smell of a musty stone cell as well as you've enjoyed the smell of a squire's kitchen, for that's what you'll be smelling next."

HAPTER 7

To officials of state, the Bastille, located at 232 Rue St. Antoine, was simply an obscure old fortress that served as a prison. But to those of us who lived near where it stood, the Bastille was much, much more. It was a castle of darkness and secrecy, a place into which one might disappear without warning, never to be heard from again. The fact that the Bastille's exterior courtyard was open to the public and that one might freely visit the gatekeeper did nothing to allay fears, for few availed themselves of such ''privileges.'' Most of us had learned at our mothers' knees the Bastille's tales of horror–tales of slimy cells overrun with rats, of vicious criminals covered with vermin and desperate for food, of cruel guards who waited for prisoners to die, then sealed them up in the thick tower walls. To put it plainly, we believed that to enter such a place was to be buried alive. You can, therefore, imagine my thoughts when Thomas and I were informed that until our trial we would be held in the Bastille.

Before the sun had set, we stood outside the fortress. The guard pushed us forward, and reluctantly we entered the prison's outer court. The gatekeeper hailed an officer, and at his command the massive drawbridge lowered and opened like a gaping wound, providing access to the inner court.

"Don't worry, Jacques," Thomas whispered in my ear as we were ushered in. "I'll think of something to get us out of here."

I said nothing.

The guard untied our hands. "Take them to the governor's quarters," he ordered one of his men who stood nearby.

I was surprised by the comfort and richness of the governor's rooms as well as by the Governor himself. Bernard René de Launay was not what I expected. He struck me as a tired man, somewhat dour to be sure, but hardly the vicious overseer I'd imagined.

"Two more for you, sir," the guard said casually.

The governor did not look up from the work before him. "What's the charge?" he demanded.

"They tried to pinch a squire of his silver."

"I can explain," said Thomas, stepping forward.

But before he could speak, the guard interjected. "He had the goods in his thieving hands when they caught him. I'd like to see him explain that."

"I was after what he owed me!" shouted Thomas, turning on the man.

"Aye," countered the guard in a cynical tone.

Without thinking, Thomas made a move toward him, and the governor was on his feet in a moment. "Enough!" he shouted, startling Thomas and giving the guard time enough to get his prisoner in a strangle hold.

"Let him go," Launay ordered after a moment. Then, addressing Thomas, he warned, "I assure you that even if you were to succeed in knocking down one of my guards, I'd have another on you in a moment."

"I meant no harm," said Thomas. "I lost my head, but if you'd let me explain–"

"Save it," the governor said, the weariness returning to his voice. "I'm sure I've heard your story before. You'll get a chance to present your case, but not to me. Until then–"

"When?" Thomas demanded. "I've a family to care for–and Jacques here has his mother."

The governor looked from one of us to the other and then he said, "You should have thought of that before."

As we were led away, I noted that the conditions were much more commonplace than I'd been led to believe. Though dark and musty, the prisoners' quarters were far from the loathsome cells of horror I had pictured.

Our cells were oddly shaped, more octagonal than square, but there was room enough for comfort in them. There were also tables and chairs provided, along with a fireplace for warmth and mats for sleeping. But these newly discovered "comforts" did little to improve my spirit. In fact, the dissipation of fear seemed only to make room for the anger I felt in being confined at all.

Of course, I told myself that my anger was directed at Latude and Thomas; it was they who had gotten me into such a mess. But even then I knew deep down, I was lying to myself. I believe it was this nagging awareness that kept me from lashing out at Thomas once we were settled in our cell.

Making my way to a corner, I sat down and propped myself against the wall–seething, sullen, and spoiling for a fight.

"Well," mused Thomas as he cautiously sat down beside me, "it's not as bad as I'd imagined."

"It's bad enough," I said.

"My wife and your mother are good, practical women," he said, perhaps trying to encourage me. "They shall see to things till we return."

I knew that his wife could manage, but my mother? She could have done so a few years before. But not now. I remembered the money Danton had given me, and I hoped that she would discover it and use it for food. I feared that she would not.

Although he did not understand why, Thomas could see that his words had only increased my misery. "Come, Jacques, they cannot keep us here long." A burst of laughter rang out and startled us. Until that moment neither Thomas nor I had noticed a third prisoner lying down in another corner of the cell.

"Are you wealthy?" the stranger asked nonchalantly.

"Oh, very!" I said, at last able to lash out at someone.

My tone had little effect upon the man, however. He sat up, stared at us for a moment, then lay back down. "No," he said with a good-naturedness that was maddening. "I can see now that you are not. And I'm sorry to say that since you are not, you may still be waiting for your trial this time next year."

I jumped to my feet and in two strides reached the man. Grabbing his collar, I hauled him up. "What do you mean!" I yelled.

Thomas quickly intervened. "Stop it, Jacques!" he said, freeing the man from my grip. "I know how you feel, but we've got to try to keep our tempers in check. It's the only way–"

"Testy, isn't he?" the man said as he relaxed again and leaned against the wall.

"He didn't mean it," Thomas said. "We're both a little testy."

"Oh, I don't mind," the stranger continued. "They're always testy when they're first brought in."

I returned to my seat feeling a bit better for having burned up some energy.

Thomas turned back to the man. "Tell me, were you serious–or just goading us–about the time it would take to get a trial?"

"I was serious," the man said, dropping his nonchalance. "I have seen artisans like you–you are artisans, aren't you?"

Thomas nodded.

"I have seen men like you wait for years."

Thomas sat down wearily.

"It need not be that way, you know," the stranger continued cautiously.

I got up and moved toward him once again, this time without anger. "What other choice do we have?" I asked.

"A boy with your spirit has many choices." Both Thomas and I moved closer to him. "I have a plan," he said, "but I cannot execute it alone."

"A plan?" said Thomas.

"I am going to escape," he said boldly.

"Can such a thing be done?" I asked.

"If you two are willing to help me," he said, "I am certain of it." He paused. "Can I count on you, or would you prefer to wait for the justice of the courts?"

The memories of my father's murder trial came flooding back to me. "You can count on me," I said.

Thomas hesitated a moment after my reply; then he added, "You can count on me as well."

CHAPTER 8

We learned that the stranger in our cell was Louis Alègre, a soldier of fortune who had endeavored to win favor at court and failed. Despite his failures as a courtier, however, he was nonetheless shrewd. As Thomas and I sat down with him the next day, we found that his plan for escape, though risky, was well thought through.

He had been imprisoned for several months. In that time he had not only learned the intricate structure of the fortress but also devised a way to construct a ladder that would prove the key to our escape.

''I have the ladder well under way,'' he told us. ''I've been making the rungs out of my firewood.''

''The weather is growing warmer,'' Thomas noted. ''They won't be giving us firewood much longer, will they?''

''They have already cut it back to just the evenings,'' Louis conceded. ''That is why I need your help. I cannot finish it with my store only. Also, if each of us takes from the store that is given to us, it will be less noticeable. We must be quick–but careful.''

''Where is this ladder?'' I inquired.

"Behind a loosened brick in the prison chapel. I go there daily and add to it as I 'pray.' " He smiled. "The guards have come to think of me as a most holy man."

"How do you keep the rungs together?" I continued.

"A friend of mine is permitted to bring me clean shirts and bed linen every week. Just before her weekly visits, I tear the shirts and linen I've been wearing all that week into strips of cloth that I can knot and restitch into sturdy rope to put between the rungs."

"Are the guards not suspicious when she brings you clean shirts and never takes the soiled ones away?" I asked.

"Oh, I leave just enough for her to wrap up as dirty laundry. Needless to say, my wardrobe is growing rather thin. I must escape if for no other reason than to replenish it."

"Incredible," Thomas said, shaking his head in disbelief.

"So we have a ladder," I said, "but what are we to do with it?"

"You are so skeptical, Jacques," said Louis smiling.

"I am growing more so," I said and cast a glance at Thomas.

"That is wise," Louis conceded. "But you must also learn to trust those who can help you, and I am one of those who can." He paused a moment and then continued. "As to your question, it is legitimate, and one I've thought about. Over these months I have–because of good behavior–been permitted to take walks in the walled garden courtyards on the towers. During these little bouts of exercise, I've been able to observe firsthand how this fortress is constructed. As anyone on the outside can see, there are eight towers, and the shape of this cell proves that we are imprisoned in one of these towers. I've learned, too, that there are five to seven stories in each tower. Most of us are confined in the middle levels. There are those few, however, who are kept in the *calottes*. Those are the levels immediately below the roof–"

I interrupted him. "What kind of prisoners are kept there?"

He shrugged. "From what I can learn, only those who are excessively violent or insane. At any rate, one of us has to get up to the *calottes* before the ladder is finished."

''What for?'' said Thomas, growing uneasy.

''To locate and examine the iron grates that I've observed on each tower roof,'' he said simply.

''How can one of us get up there if it's reserved for the violent and insane?'' I asked flatly.

''Well, Jacques,'' Louis said, ''I imagine it would be difficult for you to feign insanity–but violence?''

I was unsure at the moment if his appraisal was a compliment or insult, so I said, ''Any man can fly off in a moment of passion, but to maintain such a state–''

''Oh, you don't have to maintain it,'' he assured me. ''The guards have no notion as to your true temperament. They've seen you only a few times. I did observe, however, that one of the guards did see you collar me. We can build nicely on that first impression.''

''I'm not sure I'm all that eager to be stuck up there indefinitely.''

''It won't be indefinitely,'' he said. ''The first time they put you there, it is as a warning. I've seen them do it often. They find one of the prisoners too hotheaded, and they send him to the top of the tower for a day or two, maybe a week–no more–believing that will cure him of his temper. For the most part, it works.''

''What exactly do you want of me?'' I asked, though I was growing more uncertain about really wanting to hear his answer.

''Tonight, when the guards bring in our firewood, I want you to slug one of them.''

''Are you out of your mind?'' asked Thomas, giving voice to the very words that were on the tip of my tongue.

''It's the only way,'' Louis said simply.

''And why don't you take the chance of slugging him?'' I asked.

''Because they think of me as a holy man,'' he said. ''Besides, you do not want me to be kept from my prayers, do you?''

My concern for my mother's welfare made me desperate to escape, and seeing no other alternative, I conceded. ''All right,'' I said, ''but this had better work.''

''It will,'' Louis assured me. ''I will make certain of it, for you must not forget that my success is tied up in yours.''

HAPTER 9

With some hope before me, I was finally able to relax, and I decided to lie down for a few hours' rest before the evening came and the guards arrived.

It seemed only moments before Louis was heaving me up from a dead sleep. ''Hurry!'' he hissed.

''What–what are you–''

''The guard's in the next cell. Come on–you've got to start a fight.''

''About what?'' I staggered to my feet.

The cell door next to ours slammed shut.

Louis said nothing, fearing he'd be overheard, but his look warned me that I'd better start yelling.

''Stay on your own side of the cell,'' I shouted, just as the guard approached our door.

''Sorry,'' Louis countered, feigning an appeasing tone.

''Sorry isn't good enough,'' I screamed. The guard's key turning in our lock had brought me fully to my senses. I lunged at Louis just as the guard entered.

''Break it up!'' he ordered.

I ignored him and continued shaking Louis by the neck. ''You fool, I'll teach you who's boss here!''

As we had hoped when planning our charade, the man dropped the firewood to the floor and came at me himself. As I turned on him, however, I saw that his age was no match for my youthful strength, and I knew I had better push rather than hit him. Still, I put some muscle into it and knocked him up against the wall, then stepped back and maintained a menacing stance.

''Guards!'' he bellowed, and two more guards appeared. ''This young scoundrel needs a lesson.''

For a moment I feared that they would all three set upon me, but to my relief one of them spoke up and said, ''We'll give him some time in the *calottes*. That'll cool his temper.''

They tied my hands behind my back and led me up three flights of stairs. The damp cold and darkness increased as we ascended, and I berated myself for having left my jacket in the cell below.

When we could go no higher, they freed my hands and unlocked one of the heavy doors. Then, shoving me inside, they slammed it shut.

Darkness and the pungent smell of mold and filth overwhelmed me. I stood a moment in the center of the cell, trying to get my bearings. It was then I heard soft, squeaking sounds, and, looking down, I saw that there were several rats about my feet. Instinctively I jumped back against the wall, which sent the rodents scampering, but the feel of that slimy, lichen-covered stone against my back was even more revolting, and I quickly moved again toward the center of the room.

A low-burning torch, set in an iron ring, hung upon the wall. I took it down and slowly moved about to get a better picture of my ''room.'' I saw at once that I had finally found the Bastille that had lived in my imagination.

An old trestle table stood in one corner of the cell, and I started toward it, intending to sit down, for my heart was yet pounding in my chest. After a few steps forward, however, my heart ceased its pounding and threatened for a moment to stop altogether. Someone was already seated at the end of the table.

Louis's words about those kept in the *calottes* came back to me: "only the excessively violent or insane." The man I saw before me was indeed a strange creature. He was old, very old–and still. He sat erect, one hand resting on his knee, the other stretched out upon the table. I had never seen the likes of the shirt and breeches that he wore and concluded that they must be as old as he. But despite the worn apparel, he had the bearing of an ancient king, a monarch who had ceased his reign and had at last been cast in stone.

Assuring myself that I was certainly a match for such an aged man–no matter what his state of mind–I moved slowly forward. The light from my torch fell upon him. The long, fleecy strands of his hair and beard were thin and fine like the delicate filaments of a spider's web, and his skin, mapped with a thousand wrinkles, appeared as fragile as a butterfly's wing. But his eyes–his eyes were riveting, milky pools with black, penetrating centers. It was his eyes that made me most uneasy, for it was evident that he saw me. Yet he said not a word. Nor did I, and, unable to withstand his gaze for long, I turned and moved away.

I gave up the idea of sitting at the table and decided instead to get on with searching for a way out. I moved about the cell, scanning the ceiling for an opening which might lead to the tower roof. As far as I could see there was none. But there had to be, for Louis had insisted that he'd seen not one but several–eight to be exact–as many openings as towers.

I turned my attention to the walls themselves. The only thing I saw that held out any hope at all was the fireplace. There was no kindling, although I wished there had been, and upon inspection, I noticed that a puddle of rain water had collected at the chimney's base. Using as much light from the torch as I could, I crouched down and looked up the chimney. Sure enough, there was the iron grille leading to the roof. It would be no easy task to climb up that narrow space, but it could be done.

My discovery cheered me somewhat, and since I could do little else, I determined that I would try to get some sleep. Before I did, however, I looked back to see what the old man was doing. He sat motionless, as before. I decided that he would not give me any trouble I could not handle, and I turned my attention to finding some bedding.

There were three mattresses in the cell. Two were by the table where the old man sat; the third lay in a heap by the torch ring. I replaced the torch and then picked up the bedding, purposely avoiding examining it under the light. I was afraid that if I did so I would find it was infested with worms or lice. I soon learned–even without the light–that my fears were justified.

CHAPTER 10

I awoke abruptly to find myself clawing at my arms and legs. The lice had found me more to their taste than the filthy bedding. Jumping up, I kicked the mattress from me, but I still could not stop scratching.

"Don't scratch," a voice behind me said. Startled, I quickly turned and found myself face to face with the strange old man.

"I can't help it," I said irritably.

"You'd better," he said. "Or the sores you get will feel far worse than the itching. There is a bowl of water on the table," he continued, and he held out his gnarled hand. "Give me your clothes and go and wash yourself."

"What do you want with my clothes?" I said suspiciously.

He stared at me a moment, and I feared that he could read my thoughts of him. "Well, I certainly don't intend to wear them," he said. "You have lice."

"I imagine I'm not the only one," I replied, somewhat piqued by the comment.

"Yes, you are," he said. "I keep myself, my clothes, and my bedding clean. The man before you did not. You chose to sleep on his mattress."

''I didn't see another,'' I lied.

''Of course you did,'' he said plainly. ''You saw that there were two by me. I would have gladly given you one.''

''How was I to know that?''

''You might have asked,'' he said.

I searched his face for a hint of scorn but found there was none.

''You might have offered,'' I countered lamely.

He smiled. ''Perhaps. But I have learned I must be cautious. I need to know what kind of man–or boy–they've sent to me before I speak to him. The company they provide is not always the best.''

Without thinking, I gave vent to a derisive laugh.

''Ah, I see that they have warned you I am mad,'' he said, and turning slowly, he began to move away.

The sadness in his voice shamed me, and I quickly added, ''I believe they think us all mad.''

He turned. ''Yes,'' he said and began walking back to me. ''My name is Pierre-Joseph Aumônt.'' He bowed slightly. ''What is yours?''

''Jacques Chénier.''

''Well, Jacques,'' he said, ''it is my wash day; will you allow me to wash your suit of clothes with mine? I've only one extra set, so I must keep up with laundry.''

Deciding that there was no better way to rid myself of lice, I slipped out of my shirt and breeches and gave them to him.

He accepted the bundle with great care, holding them as far away as possible.

''You can slip on my old cloak until these things are dry–that is *after* you have washed,'' he said. ''You'll find it lying on the chair.''

I watched him as he started off toward a corner of the room where I saw he had prepared a basin of water that he had set atop a small paving stone. A feeble coal fire glowed beneath the stone.

I was surprised that I'd noticed neither the stone nor the basin the night before, but I suppose the rats, the madman, and chimney had so diverted my attention that I saw little else.

When he reached the basin, he left my belongings in a heap while he set about wringing out his own laundry, which had been soaking in the pot. When he finished, he took up my clothes and dropped them in.

He then pulled from his pocket several bits of bread crust and moved to the center of the room. Stooping down, he began to whistle softly. I was horrified to see the rats coming out from the corners in answer to his call.

''What are you doing?'' I shouted.

He looked up at me. ''Feeding the rats.'' Then, noting the panic on my face, he added, ''I have found that if I feed them, they are not compelled to feed on me.''

I stood gawking until I began to shiver. I then decided that it was time to begin washing. As I did, I wondered whether this frail old man was unusually clever or simply mad. I decided that in such a place as the Bastille they could well seem the same. Still, I wondered what circumstances could have brought him to this place, for though he was old, his bearing, his manner, and even his worn suit of clothes revealed that he had once been a gentleman.

The ice-cold water in the bowl numbed me, and by the time I threw Pierre-Joseph's cloak about my shoulders, the itching had somewhat subsided.

''How long have you been here?'' I asked, sitting down at the table, for the cloak reminded me that I had never seen such clothes before.

He stopped his work and paused a moment as if he were trying hard to remember. ''I've little way of knowing,'' he finally said. ''All that I can say is that when I came here, I was much younger–'' he looked down at his gnarled hands ''–and stronger. I remember, too, that the Sorbonne Library had just opened and that an astonishing boy named Mozart had come to the city to play for the elite of Paris.'' A vague smile crossed his face. ''Paris was a gay city then. Is it yet?''

''For some it is,'' I said. I'd never heard of Mozart, but the Sorbonne Library had been open for as long as I could remember. I tried again. ''This Mozart, did he play at court for the king and queen?''

''For Louis XV? Not that I remember.''

''Louis *XV*?''

He paused, and then asked, ''He is dead then?''

''Yes,'' I said. ''His grandson now sits on the throne, Louis XVI. Does no one speak to you?''

''You are the first person that I've had a real conversation with since–well, I can't remember. The men who are placed here with me are often drunk or violent. They do not care for conversation. I used to try to talk, but I learned that to do so was at best unwise. I suppose that is one reason they think me mad. Silence frightens people.''

''Why did you decide to talk with me?'' I asked.

''I watched you. You were neither drunk nor violent–which makes me wonder why you were put up here at all.''

I could feel my face redden under his gaze. ''I lost my temper,'' was all I said.

Noting my reticence, he changed the subject. ''How long ago did Louis die?''

''The year after I was born,'' I said.

He nodded as he took the information in. ''And how old are you?'' he asked.

''Fifteen–almost sixteen.''

He was silent. After a moment, he turned slowly and resumed his task.

As I continued watching him, the realization that this old man had been imprisoned for at least as long as I had been alive began sinking in. No wonder he was mad–or was he? I had certainly met greater fools–perhaps even greater madmen. I wanted to ask what horrid crime he had committed that kept him in this place, but he had been kind enough not to press me for information, and I knew I owed him the same.

Looking about for something to divert my attention, I spotted an object lying at the other end of the table. I reached over and picked it up. It seemed to be an iron bar with crude holes bored into it.

"Do you use this to protect yourself from the other prisoners?" I asked, holding up what I thought to be a weapon.

He turned, and seeing what was in my hand, he broke into a soft but merry laugh.

Somewhat chagrined by his response, I said, "It certainly doesn't look good for much else."

He ceased his laughter. "You don't think much of my handiwork."

"Tell me what it is," I demanded. "Perhaps then I'll change my mind."

"It is my flute," he said.

I looked at him, dumbfounded.

"I know it looks a bit primitive, but it plays well enough."

"However did you make it?" I asked.

"I did it many years ago when I first came to this place. Those first few days were terrible." He shook his head. "My hope revived the day after my arrival when I received a parcel from the guard. It was an extra suit of clothes. He would not tell me who had brought them, but I hoped that whoever it was would also return with books and possibly my flute. But as the days passed, I realized that all I would have to amuse myself would be what I brought with me: one Book–which I had about me when I was taken–and my ingenuity. I decided I could use the latter to make myself a flute. I took a crossbar from that trestle table; I'm sure you've noticed it's unsteady."

He smiled at the thought before continuing. "I beat and fashioned it into a crude knife. Then I got one of the hollow bars from that iron grate at the chimney's base over there, and after much patience succeeded in boring holes in it. As I have said, I was stronger then."

"The guards did not try to stop you?"

He smiled. "I think they were afraid to try. I later learned that they thought my frantic pounding was simply madness."

"But surely when you'd finished they could see what you had done," I said.

"As you will recall," he reminded me, "you did not think much of my work when you first saw it."

"I'm sure you told them–as you did me–what it was you'd made."

"I did," he said. "I even played it for them, but you will find that first impressions die hard. They were less afraid to bring in my supper but fearful enough to keep alive the idea that I was mad. Still," he sighed contentedly, "I had my flute."

By this time he had finished with the wash and joined me at the table.

"What kind of songs do you play?" I asked.

"My own," he said. "I was quite a good musician in my youth."

"They must be sad songs."

"What makes you think so?"

"What other kind of songs could you write in such a place as this?" I asked.

"Music reflects what's in the heart; not what is in one's surroundings."

"And what is that–what is in your heart, I mean?"

"I told you that I had one Book with me. I have spent these years hiding that Book in my heart, and I would like to think that my music in some measure reflects the peace that I have found there."

"Peace?" I said. "After the disgrace of imprisonment for all these years, how can you talk of peace when–" I hesitated, "when everyone believes you mad?"

"I have ceased to care what others think of me," he said. "Of course, there was a time when that was not the case, but I have since learned that it is my heart, not my circumstances, that determines whether I am a man of honor or disgrace. The longer you live, Jacques, the more you will see that many of those held in honor are fools and that those counted as foolish are the wisest of men. The Book I speak of," he continued, "is more than just a book to me. You might say, it is part of my heritage. It has been in my family for over a hundred years."

"Your family," I said, taking an opportunity to learn more of him, "have they not been able in all these years to get your release?"

"As far as I know, they never knew that I was here," he said.

I waited for him to tell me more. When he did not, I asked, "May I see your book?"

He looked at me for what seemed a long time. "You may, if you promise that you will tell no one that I have it."

"The guards do not mind your flute; why would they mind your having a book?"

"I do not know if they would mind or not; but I will take no chance of losing it."

"All right," I said, "I promise."

He got up, went to the corner of the cell, and after rummaging under his bedding, pulled out a small but rather thick book. He brought it over, holding it in both hands, carefully but securely, as I would have held a new-made sculpture in which I took pride.

"Can you read?" he asked, as he returned and sat beside me.

"Of course," I said. "Artisans know how to read."

"Good," he said smiling. Then he began carefully thumbing through the delicate pages. "While I play for you, you can read the words that inspired my song. You shall see it is not sad." Handing me the book, he showed me the place. I looked down as he began to play:

Everyone who thirsts,
Come to the waters;

And you who have no money,
Come, buy and eat.
Why do you spend money for what is not bread,
And your wages for what does not satisfy?
Listen carefully to Me, and eat what is good,
And let your soul delight itself in abundance.
Incline your ear, and come to me.
Hear, and your soul shall live.
Seek the Lord while he may be found,
Call upon Him while He is near.
Let the wicked forsake his way,
And the unrighteous man his thoughts;
Let him return to the Lord,
And He will have mercy on him;
And to our God, for he will abundantly pardon.
For thus says the High and Lofty One
Who inhabits eternity, whose name is Holy:
"I dwell in the high and holy place,
With him who has a contrite and humble spirit,
To revive the spirit of the humble,
And to revive the heart of the contrite ones."

The beauty of the words, the music, the scent of the Book's soft leather cover, and the feel of its delicate pages made me forget the musty, darkened cell until Pierre-Joseph broke off his music in haste. One of the guards was coming toward the cell. Quickly I closed the Book and gave it back to him. He had barely put it in its place before the guard came in with two bowls of gruel.

"You better watch out for him," the guard said, as he set down the bowls and started out. But when he reached the door, he turned, and, pointing to Pierre-Joseph, he added, "He's a sly one he is. He may be calm for now, but sometime when you're not looking–" he broke off his speech and made a mocking gesture as if to slit his throat.

I am ashamed to say that I said nothing in defense of this man who had been so kind to me. Instead, I simply watched the guard as he went out, shaking his head and laughing to himself.

HAPTER 11

I am certain that the guards would have been disappointed had they known that my stay in the *calottes* was not the "horror" they intended. Indeed, as I was taken from the cell several days later, I found myself regretting my departure. I was, of course, glad to leave the rats and filth behind, but I was also saddened to leave the "mad" Pierre, for there was much about him–and his treasured Book–that yet intrigued me.

I was still thinking on Pierre-Joseph and on all of my unanswered questions when I entered my old cell. Thomas and Louis were seated at the table, but as soon as the guard closed and locked the door, they were both upon me.

"Well?" said Louis.

"Well what?" I asked.

"The opening–can we get out?" Thomas prodded.

"Oh!" I said, remembering my mission. "Well–we must go up through the chimney. It won't be easy–"

"But it's possible?" Louis interrupted.

"Yes," I said. "It's possible."

"Good! Come, sit down."

''The ladder's done,'' Thomas informed me, as we gathered round the table.

''No more need for praying now,'' Louis laughed.

''Unless it be for rain,'' said Thomas.

''Nature will take care of that,'' Louis assured him. ''Spring is here, and with spring the rains will come.''

''Why do we need rain?'' I asked.

''To get rid of the night guards who walk atop the towers,'' Louis said. ''The sentries do not make their rounds if it is raining.''

''Where is the ladder? Still in the chapel?'' I asked.

Louis shook his head and smiled. Then, motioning for Thomas to watch the door, he moved to the corner of the room and began rummaging amidst his bedding, which was piled up against the wall. Pulling out an unwieldy bundle, he brought it to the table.

''I'm not sure you will be able to get that bulging thing up the chimney,'' I warned him.

''Oh, don't worry, I'll just unwind it a bit,'' he said. ''Believe me, there's a way. I've not come this far only to allow such a trivial thing to deter me. Do you know what I call it?'' he continued enthusiastically. ''I call it Jacob's ladder; after all it was kept in a chapel.'' He began to laugh as he fumbled with the bundle. ''I've been six months in making this.''

''How long is the thing?'' I asked, astonished as he began unwinding it.

''About three hundred feet I'd guess.''

He yanked and pulled on the ropes that bound the rungs together, smiling broadly at how well it held. Then, satisfied that he'd secured my admiration, he rewrapped his handiwork and placed it behind the heap of bedding by the wall.

''By the way,'' Louis said, as he and Thomas returned to their seats at the table. ''What was it like up there?''

''The cell itself was as bad as it could get–all that we had feared,'' I said, pointing my remark to Thomas.

"Did you see anyone else up there?" asked Louis.

"Just an old man," I said.

"Must be an old lunatic–" said Thomas, moving closer. "Was he frightening too?"

"Hardly," I said. Then, turning to Louis, I inquired, "Do you know who he might be?"

"I have heard there is one old madman they keep up there. There's not much more to tell," he said, "except that he's been here more than twenty years. No one knows just why. I imagine they have all forgotten. There are tales, though, that he's violent when provoked."

"He hasn't enough strength for violence," I said scornfully. "Any young man could get the upper hand, at least in a battle of fists."

"But not in a battle of wits, huh?" Louis laughed.

"It's hard to say," I continued, ignoring his laughter. "He seems to have been well educated in his time and is quite the gentleman despite his horrid living conditions. That's what puzzles me. He looks as if he had his share of money once. Why didn't he buy his freedom?"

Louis shrugged. "Maybe his money ran out."

"Perhaps," I said. "Still, I've been thinking–" I hesitated.

"What?" coaxed Thomas.

"Well, since we must exit from the *calottes,* could we not take him with us?"

"An old lunatic! You *have* spent too much time with him," said Louis. "You've lost your mind as well!"

"I could see to him," I said, not at all sure that I really could.

"You didn't tell him of our plan did you?" Louis queried.

"Of course not," I assured him.

"Besides, Jacques," Thomas interjected, "we've no assurance that we'll exit through his cell. Louis tells me that there are many cells up there."

"Come to think of it," I said, "how are we all three going to get up to the *calottes* at the same time?"

"That's easy enough," said Louis. "We'll get in such a row that they will be forced to throw us up there in order to get any peace."

"What if they put us into different cells?" questioned Thomas.

"They won't," Louis assured him. "I've conducted experiments with several other cell mates."

"Experiments?" I asked.

He nodded, a look of pride upon his face. "I'd pit one against another, subtly you understand, so that they had no notion I was doing so. Then I'd watch them break into a brawl. They were always taken up to the *calottes* and always to the same cell. The guards kept them together so that they could fight it out without disturbing anyone."

"Why did you not tell those other prisoners of your plans?" I asked.

"Because I was nowhere near finished with the ladder."

"So we got in on it by the luck of the draw, you might say," said Thomas.

"You might say that," said Louis. "Of course, I sized you up a bit as well," he added.

"And if we had not measured up?" I asked.

"Then I would have waited until they brought the next batch of prisoners in," he said. "Unlike you, Jacques, I'm a patient man. A month or two more would have meant little to me."

"What are we to do now?" I asked, feeling that there must be something that could occupy our time.

"Sit and wait for rain, as I have said."

"What you haven't said," I reminded him, making no effort to conceal my irritation at his flippant tone, "is how we are to know it is raining. We are in the center of a tower with three levels of stone overhead."

He got up, walked to the corner of the room, and sat down to lean against his mass of wadded bedding. ''That friend of mine who does my laundry, she will not come again until a storm is raging.''

I got up and began to pace about the room; life in a cell was once more pressing down on me. I wanted out–now. For whenever I stopped long enough to ponder, I remembered my mother and her desperate need of me.

''Relax, Jacques,'' Thomas said. ''Your pacing will not make it rain.''

''Perhaps not,'' I said, ''but it will help me endure this place until it does.''

CHAPTER 12

The spring rains were later than usual, and it was three miserable weeks before we finally heard the welcome words from Louis's friend: "The weather is frightful." As the guard ushered her in, she added, "I almost didn't come."

"I'm glad you did," said Louis, carefully framing his conversation, for the guard had remained just outside the door. "I'm in desperate need of clean shirts."

"Well, you need not have waited for me," she said. "You could have hung them outside for a thorough washing. Not only is the rain coming down in buckets, but the wind is whipping up something fierce."

"Perhaps it will stop by evening?" Louis asked pointedly.

"That's not likely," she reassured him. "The sky looks as if it will be rumbling all night. I'd say tomorrow's dawn will be the first sign of clearing."

"Well, the weather affects us little here," Louis said. He went to retrieve several old shirts for her–whole shirts this time.

"Well, I mustn't stay," she said, as she stuffed them into her basket. "I've yet to run my errands."

He bent to kiss her hand. "Until next week, then?"

"Or before," she replied with a knowing smile.

As soon as the guard was out of sight, Thomas asked the very question that was on my lips, "Tonight? It is tonight then?"

"Tonight it is," said Louis.

"How soon do we start up a brawl?" I asked impatiently.

"Let us first map out last-minute plans," he said, motioning us to the table. "Then we shall give them such a brawl that they'll be forced to shut us up in the *calottes* for weeks!"

* * *

The row that we invented went perfectly–as rows go. In moments, several guards came barging in. "Break it up! Break it up!" they shouted as they pulled us off one another.

"You never learn, do you?" said the one who collared me.

"Leave us to our fighting," shouted Louis. "It won't be settled until I knock both of them senseless!" he added for good effect.

"We'll see about that," Thomas chimed in. I decided not to join them; this being my second offense, I knew that I was already on my way upstairs. I feared to push my luck further.

"If you two don't keep quiet, I'll throw you both up upstairs with this young rascal. Then you can all three rot together for a few days!"

"That suits me fine!" said Louis, with a sincerity that I feared was telling.

At this point, Thomas broke away from the guard that was holding him and lunged at Louis. That clinched it. "Round them all up," bellowed the guard at the door. "If we're lucky they will kill each other, and we can save on gruel and kindling."

Louis feigned the cooling of his temper and convinced the guard to relax his grip long enough for him to scoop up his bundle of "belongings" to take with him. His reputation must have aided him, for neither Thomas nor I were afforded such a privilege, and for the second time I was hauled off without my jacket.

I was both relieved and disappointed that we were not put in Pierre-Joseph's cell. I had thought much of him over the past weeks. I had not, however, been able to come up with a realistic solution for including him in our plans, and I could not imagine facing him without asking him to come along.

By the time we reached the *calottes* I was feeling the effects of our fray in earnest. My lower lip had swelled to twice its size, and my nose had started spouting blood like one of the fountains in the Tuileries gardens.

''I think you two got a bit carried away down there,'' I said, when at last we'd been left alone again.

''Had to make it look like the real thing,'' said Louis, with that implacable calm that over the weeks had begun to drive me to distraction.

''From the looks of Thomas and the bleeding of my nose, it *was* the real thing.'' I said, as I forced my head back in an effort to stop my nosebleed.

''How'd you come out without a scratch?'' Thomas inquired sullenly. He too had noticed that Louis barely looked rumpled, let alone battle scarred.

''Because I am as wily as I am patient,'' he said. ''So this is our way out, huh, Jacques?'' He began his examination of the chimney.

''That's it,'' I said. ''Not very inviting but–''

He cut me off. ''What's at the top will make it worth it.''

''The top of the tower's just the start,'' interjected Thomas. ''We've still got to get down the tower and across the moat,'' he reminded Louis. ''Or have you forgotten those hurdles?''

''Small hurdles, Thomas,'' Louis said, ''for we have Jacob's ladder.'' He patted the bundle that lay beside him.

''I'd feel better if they'd just let us out the front gate and across the drawbridge,'' Thomas sighed.

I agreed with Thomas.

''There would be no adventure in that,'' chided Louis.

My nosebleed had finally abated, and Thomas and I joined him at the chimney's base.

"Well, when do we begin this big adventure?" asked Thomas.

"No time like the present, for I'm sure the night has fallen," said Louis. Then he turned to me. "Now, Jacques, once you get to the top–"

"Once *I* get to the top?" I interrupted. "What makes you think I'm going to be the first one to stuff myself up that chimney? *You're* the mastermind behind this plan, remember. You can have the honor."

"You're going to be the first one," explained Louis in a most condescending tone, "because you are the lankiest. You are the only one of us that is lean enough to wedge himself in that space and climb up to the top. Once you're there, you should be able to loosen the grate with little difficulty. I've examined them as I've walked atop the towers; they're not secured by any means."

"Guess they never thought anyone would be dumb enough to try to crawl up the chimney," said Thomas.

"I wonder why?" I asked sarcastically.

I realized, however, that there was no way of arguing myself out of forging the way. So, anxious to get it over with as quickly as possible, I moved into position. "Don't forget the ladder," I said.

"Oh, you must take it with you," Louis informed me as he handed it over. "When you get onto the roof, you let it down a bit and use it to haul Thomas and me up. Don't worry," he added as he shoved me toward the opening, "I'll do my best to push you up as far as I can."

"Thanks," I said, snatching the bundle from him.

"Good luck, Jacques," I heard Thomas say as I stuck my head into the chimney.

The rain was leaking in, making an already dreadful task even worse. I placed my back against one side of the chimney wall, and with Louis's help I managed to draw my knees up to my chest and place my feet against the opposite wall. The ladder was cradled–or crammed–into my lap.

I felt the panic rising and I stopped a moment to breathe deeply. "What's wrong?" asked Louis.

"Nothing," I said. "Just give me a minute."

"Sure," he said. "Just tell me when you're ready for a push."

I leaned my head back and closed my eyes. The inch or two on either side of my shoulders helped to quell my fear. *You've got a bit of room,* I reasoned with myself. *Not much, but enough.*

My muscles began cramping up. Like it or not, I knew I had to get moving. "Push," I ordered, and Louis gave a heave–and then another–and a large clot of loosened soot fell down upon me.

I can hardly relate the horror that I felt as that wet, suffocating mess covered my face. "Stop!" I managed to choke out. "Stop!"

"Jacques, Jacques," I could hear Thomas calling.

"He's all right," Louis reassured him. "Shake your head, Jacques. Get the soot out of your face."

His voice, though right below me, sounded as if it were coming from the end of a long tunnel. I imagine I was close to blacking out, but I heard enough to obey. Once I was able to brush the filthy substance from my face, I revived somewhat.

"Just breathe deeply for a few moments," Louis continued. "I'm sure the worst of it is loosened now. We'll take it slower. Just tell me when you're ready."

I desperately wanted to turn back, but I knew that I could not, and, steeling myself against my fear, I started slowly upward. Louis sensed my movement and did what he could to aid me.

It seemed hours before I reached the top. By the time I did, the muscles in my legs and back were nearly numb with aching, and my hands were cold and stiff. The thunder roared as I reached up and grabbed the grate, desperately hoping that it would give without much effort. It did. I managed to push it to one side, and, clinging to the edge of the opening, I pulled with all my strength to lift myself up a bit. After forcing my body into what seemed every conceivable contortion, I finally managed to roll out onto the roof. Flinging the bundle aside, I lay there for a moment with the rain beating down on me, my limbs stretched out to their full length.

A flash of lightning brought me to my senses and reminded me that if I were seen, my troubles would be multiplied tenfold.

Quickly I unwrapped the ladder, let it down, and waited until I felt a firm grip at the other end. I then began to pull. By the time I saw Thomas's smiling face, I had used my last ounce of strength.

"You'll have to get Louis up," I said, collapsing into a heap.

"Of course," said Thomas. "Save what breath you have left. You'll need it for the trip down the side of the tower."

Louis was out on the tower roof and ready to go on much sooner than I'd wished. "Keep low," he said as we moved to the parapet.

Cautiously he peered over the edge. "Well, it looks as if it's as quiet as it's going to get."

He threw the ladder over and anchored it around one of the jutting rows of bricks along the tower's ledge.

The panic in me began to rise again as I saw the long drop into the moat. The ladder looked ludicrously flimsy as it blew and twisted in the wind and rain. "Are you sure that thing will hold us?" I asked.

"So sure," said Louis, "that I will be the first one to descend it." And, throwing his leg over the wall, he started down.

Despite the height, I found that getting down the ladder was far easier than climbing out onto the roof. Louis, for all his faults, had made a flawless piece of work. So flawless in fact, that he was loath to leave it. "It is hard to leave behind such a rare and precious monument to human industry," he said as we pressed ourselves against the base of the tower wall, shivering in the moat.

"Come on," I said, kicking out from the wall, "this is no time for sentimentality."

''How can you be so callous to cast aside, without regret, the tools that helped us to our liberty?'' Louis continued his lament as we swam to the other side. It was obvious he had worked less than I, for I had neither wind nor strength for conversation.

Thomas was losing patience as well. ''Keep it down,'' he said. ''We're not out of this yet.''

''Look,'' I said, pointing up at the tower. We had been so intent upon getting through the moat that we failed to notice that the rain had stopped. The sentries had resumed their rounds, armed as usual with broad lanterns.

''What now?'' hissed Thomas, for we had reached the other side.

''Get out,'' Louis said. We obeyed.

''Now, crawl–staying on your stomach–until you reach the gate. There are no sentries in the outer courtyard at night. They are too confident of their moat. If we make it that far, we'll be free.''

''If!'' I said it quietly, but with all the anger in my voice that I could muster. ''It's a good 200 yards over stones and who knows what else–on our stomachs?''

''Would you like to turn around?'' Louis asked.

I put my face down to the dirt and started crawling.

HAPTER 13

By the time we reached the outer courtyard, I was a matted mess of dirt, bruises, and bloodstains. But once outside that gate in the haven of a darkened street, I felt an exhilaration that I can scarcely put into words. Thomas and I were both eager to get home and paused only a moment before setting out in the direction of our shops.

Louis quickly followed after us. ''Where do you two think you're going?''

''Home,'' said Thomas, without glancing back.

''Oh, that is brilliant,'' Louis said, and his derisive tone pulled us to a stop.

''What do you mean?'' I said.

''You're going home? To do what? Wait until morning when the guards discover that you have escaped and come to fetch you back to prison?''

''Do you have a better idea?'' asked Thomas.

''Of course, he does,'' I said. ''He always has–''

Thomas cut me off. ''Let's hear him out,'' he said.

"My friend," Louis began. "She lives in St. Germain. Her father is a tailor; he will give us shelter for the night."

"And tomorrow?" Thomas asked.

"Tomorrow he has promised to get me safely into the Low Countries. I'm sure that he can do the same for you."

"The Low Countries?" I said. "We can't leave Paris."

"Jacques is right," Thomas said. "I've a wife and son to care for."

"And how do you intend to care for them?" asked Louis. "Where else can a cabinetmaker and a sculptor find work in Paris but in St. Antoine, and I am telling you it is not safe for you to work there."

I could see Thomas wavering. "We'll manage," I said.

"How, Jacques?" questioned Thomas. "Louis is right. We're not thinking clearly."

"And he is?" I said sarcastically. "How can we support ourselves by fleeing Paris? Tell me that."

"I have connections," Louis said. "I already know that there will be work waiting for me. I will see that you find jobs as well."

"Why this sudden interest in our future? Inside the prison, you made it clear that we were chosen simply as a matter of convenience. Why exactly do you want us to go along now?" I said, trying to find something that would help me change Thomas's mind.

"You helped me escape. I like to pay my debts. Besides, if they find you, it will go very badly for you. And though I admit that I am prone to look to my own interests first, I am not averse to looking out for others when I can."

"How will we get the money that we make back to our families?" Thomas questioned, genuinely interested now.

"I have arrangements for that as well. I can also see that your families are notified of our plans, though I insist that they do not know our exact location."

I felt Thomas's gaze upon me, but I could not face him. I knew that I had no choice. I could not leave my mother, and though I knew it was unfair of me, I desperately wanted Thomas to return to St. Antoine as well. ''Jacques?'' he finally said.

I could hold out no longer. ''I must stay here,'' I said. ''But you go on. I'll tell your family that you'll be in touch.''

''You're sure?'' Thomas asked. ''Your mother would understand.''

''I'm sure,'' I said.

''Goodbye, Jacques,'' Louis said, offering his hand. ''You have spirit. If anyone can survive as a fugitive in Paris, you can.''

I took his hand then, and said farewell to Thomas.

It was well into the night, but my shop was not far. When I reached it, I remembered that I'd left my key in my jacket pocket. Fortunately, I had long ago seen the necessity of preparing for emergencies and had done so by putting a clump of molding wax inside our shop bell and pressing an extra key into the wax. I reached up now and retrieved it, congratulating myself on my ingenuity.

The shop was dark, but despite the blackness, I could feel that I was home. I stood for a moment, taking in the smell of my leather aprons, molding clay, wax, and chiseled stone. Then, running my hand across the scarred surface of my wooden worktable, I found the cool, smooth form of my iron tools. I realized then just how much I'd missed the feel of them.

I found a candle and got it burning. As the light fell on the worktable, I saw that the money I'd left there so many weeks ago was gone. I took comfort in the fact, forcing myself to believe that my mother had spent it on food, not wine.

Heading up the stairs, I told myself that perhaps the fear brought on by my abrupt departure and the joy my mother would feel in knowing of my safe return might be enough to rekindle in her the desire to be the mother she once was.

Once upstairs, I made my way across the room as quietly as possible, for I did not want to startle her. Then, setting the candle on the table, I carefully pulled back the curtain and called softly, ''Mother–''

She was gone.

I ran downstairs, out into the alley, and down to Thomas's shop. I banged upon the door and kept on banging until I saw the light of a lantern through the glass. I could see Phillipe and his mother cautiously approaching. "Open up, Madame Grammônd. It's me, Jacques," I called in to her.

Hearing my name, Phillipe ran ahead of his mother and opened up the door.

"Jacques!" he shouted.

His mother was quickly at his side. "Jacques, how–"

"My mother," I said. "I've just gone home. She isn't there."

I waited for an answer, but Phillipe and his mother just stood there staring.

"Surely, you saw her leave. Someone must have–"

"Jacques," Madame Grammônd interrupted; then she paused a moment. "I'm sorry," she finally said.

"Sorry?" I said, the truth beginning to weigh down on me.

Phillipe stood beside his mother, but he would no longer look up at me.

"I didn't know she needed help," his mother endeavored to explain. "Phillipe, he tried–two weeks or more had passed before I noticed that he'd been taking loaves of bread from the kitchen. I followed him one day to see that he was leaving them at your shop door–"

"The door was locked," he said, still refusing to look up. "I couldn't take the bread in to her. I rang the bell, but she never answered. I thought of telling Mama, but I–I didn't think you'd want me to."

His mother put out her hand to comfort him. "He did what he thought best, Jacques. He piled the bread up outside the door every day, hoping she would see it. She never did–the pigs would end up eating it. When I finally realized what he was doing, I went down to her myself. I banged and banged–and then began to worry. I got the locksmith to let me inside–but it was too late." Her voice dropped almost to a whisper. "She must have starved."

I stood there, stunned into silence, until I heard her voice once again. "Jacques, I know this may not be the time, but–I must ask; have you news of Thomas?"

I told her all I knew, then, still numbed by what I'd learned, I turned and made my way back to my shop.

I walked through the open door and slowly went back up the stairs. The half-open curtains hung like a shroud about her bed, and on the table, I saw my candle's dying flame mirrored in one of the wine bottles she had cast aside. The sight of it awakened my dulled senses, and rushing to the table, I picked up the bottle and hurled it crashing to the wall. "I hate you!" I shouted. The years of seething anger at last erupted in fury, a fury that could not be quenched without revenge. "De Guiche–Latude–all of you. I'll kill you if I ever get the chance!"

I turned in search of something else to hurl but saw instead the small shadow of Phillipe standing on the stairs. I stopped. He came to me and gently took my hand in his. In that moment of stillness he looked up at me. "I will hate them too," he said.

CHAPTER 14

That night as Phillipe and I sat in the shop together, I struggled to turn my thoughts to surviving as a fugitive in Paris. My only means of livelihood was my shop. I could not, would not, give it up. Despite the risk, I determined that I would continue as a sculptor in St. Antoine, and I set my mind to devising a plan that would enable me to do so.

''I need your help, Phillipe,'' I said to him. He nodded. ''I'm going to make several busts and statues of the philosophers, princes–all the popular faces I've done before. When I'm finished, I want you to take them to Charpentier's café.''

''You want me to sell them for you?''

''No,'' I said. ''You will be my legs to deliver the work, but Charpentier shall be my eyes to seek out a clientele.''

''But what am I to tell Monsieur Charpentier if he asks why you have not come to the café yourself?''

''If he does not already know, you can tell him what happened to your father and me. He'll understand why I must remain in hiding. Tell him that I will give him a portion of my commissions; enough to pay him for the time he takes on my behalf and for any inconvenience he may encounter in keeping my whereabouts a secret."

"When do you want me to go?"

"Tomorrow," I said. "You can explain our plans to him then. I will also try to have at least one thing finished for you to take along. I'm going to work the rest of the night–and every night while Paris sleeps. You can come each morning a little before sunrise and collect what I have finished."

"Will you work all day as well?" he asked.

"No. During the day I will have to lose myself among the hordes of beggars in the streets. No one must know that I have been in this shop. You understand?"

"Yes," he said, "but when will you sleep–and eat?"

"Whenever and wherever I can."

A worried frown creased his brow. "I will bring you bread when I come," he said.

"I will sleep–and eat–Phillipe. Don't worry."

"I'll bring you bread," he said dogmatically.

"Just tomorrow," I conceded. "Come an hour or so before dawn and we will eat together." The proposal cheered him. "Go home for now. You will have only a couple of hours' sleep as it is."

I led him out and stood watching until he disappeared into his shop.

I stood alone in the alley, unwilling to go back inside my shop, reluctant to face all the bitter–and sweet–memories that were housed within. I was certain that our escape from the Bastille was as yet undetected. Perhaps I could still risk a walk through the city as a free man. I set out and soon found myself walking once again along the Seine.

The air was cool and the sound of the water's ebb and flow soothing–but not as soothing as it had been when I walked along the cobbled wharf so many weeks before. How much had happened since that night when I first saw Danton at Charpentier's! At that time, I believed that with my father's death the Comte de Guiche's murderous son had taken all there was to take from me.

How wrong I was. Now I had lost my mother too, and in my mind, the young nobleman stood convicted of that crime as well. Had my father lived, my mother would have lived also. As I thought upon these things, any peace that still remained in my heart departed from me, and gazing down into the river, I felt as if the secret of the Seine's calm constancy was locked away from me forever. I turned toward home, determined to hold fast to the only solace left me–my work.

Entering the shop, I closed the door and locked it. Then, moving over to my worktable, I discovered the unfinished portrait of Danton lying just as I had left it. It startled me at first to see his face again. I picked up the medallion and examined it. As I did so, it occurred to me that Danton had been wise to demand the work in wax, for wax remained somewhat pliable. Like Danton, with a bit of heat, it could be transformed in a moment. Only a fool would have chosen to cast such a man in stone.

I could see that the work I'd done was true–at least in part. I had captured Danton as an orator, a champion of the people. His speech came readily back to mind. It was true that the rich lived extravagantly and the poor paid for it in taxes. It had always been so. Perhaps Danton was a wiser man than I'd believed him to be. Even if he himself did not understand poverty, he understood its cause. I gazed at his image before me and knew that it would please him. I determined that I would finish the medallion that night, for I remembered that he had already paid me for half of the commission.

* * *

Phillipe arrived an hour or so before dawn, a loaf of bread under each arm. I took the bread from him and set it on the table. "You have told your mother of our plans?" I asked, as I handed the medallion to him.

"Yes," he said. "She is glad that I can help." He looked down at the medallion in his hand and asked, "Why did you make this?"

"It was an unfinished commission," I said. "This is what Danton wanted the night he came here. Charpentier knows of it. I only hope that Danton still visits the café, but even if he doesn't, perhaps Charpentier knows where to find him. You can at least ask if it can be delivered."

"All right," he said. Then, shaking his head, he added, "I can't see why he would ever want a picture of himself."

"He said it was for a lady." Phillipe looked doubtful. "I had my doubts as well," I confessed, "but that *is* what he told me. Come. We'd best get to eating what you brought. It will be light soon, and we must both be gone."

I spent that day wandering the back streets of St. Germain, for I felt no urge to sleep. I suppose what drew me to St. Germain was the faint hope that Thomas and Louis would still be there somewhere, but I saw no trace of them. I toyed with the idea of searching out the tailor whom Louis had claimed as friend, but thought better of it. There were almost as many tailors in St. Germain as brewers, and I could not risk asking questions of just anyone. Still, such thoughts gave a vague purpose to my wandering. I was glad when darkness finally fell and I could make my way back to St. Antoine.

Phillipe was faithful to come just at the time I'd told him.

"Were you able to deliver the medallion?" I asked when he had settled himself on a stool.

"Yes, and I've got the other half of the commission for you too," he said, digging into the ragged pocket of his breeches and pulling out the money.

"This is more than he owed me," I said. "Are you sure there is no mistake?"

Phillipe shrugged. "He said to give it to you. He said he was glad to pay for such work as yours even if he didn't really want the medallion anymore."

"He didn't want it?" I asked.

"That's what he said."

"What was wrong with it?"

''Nothing,'' Phillipe assured me. ''He liked it well enough. But he said to tell you that he'd already won the lady's heart.''

''Why ever did he take it then?'' I asked.

''He wants to show it to a friend of his, a man he thinks can help you.''

''Help me? How? You did not tell him I am working here.''

A look of indignation came into his childish face. ''Of course I didn't.''

''I'm sorry,'' I said. ''Go on. Help me how?''

''Danton said that he came here looking for you when you failed to show at Charpentier's. When he saw the shop deserted, he decided to get someone else to do the work. The man he found lives on the Boulevard. He has a *cabinet* of waxworks there. Danton said that he is going to show the man your medallion and he thinks it will impress him. He can give you steady work.''

''Does Charpentier know of this man?''

''Yes,'' Phillipe said. ''I asked him what he thought of him.''

''What did he say?''

''He said, 'Tell Jacques that he can trust Danton's advice.' I like Charpentier well enough,'' Phillipe continued unbidden, ''but, Danton–I still don't like him much.''

''Still, I need to make a living,'' I said. ''If I decide to accept, how am I to meet this man?''

Phillipe looked down and assumed a look of strained concentration. ''Tomorrow afternoon at three o'clock,'' he began slowly, as if he were struggling to remember the message just as it had been given. ''You are to meet Danton on the boulevard next to the theater where the marionettes perform.'' He looked up again, a smile on his face. ''That is just what he said.''

I returned his smile, but continued to weigh the content of his message. ''I suppose if Charpentier says he's trustworthy, it is worth the risk,'' I said at length. ''I only hope that Charpentier knows Danton as well as he thinks he does.''

''He should,'' Phillipe remarked.

"Why? Does he go to the café often now?"

"Every day."

"Charpentier has taken to him then," I said, "or he would not encourage it."

"He has more than taken to him," Phillipe informed me.

"What do you mean?"

"Danton has married Charpentier's daughter."

"Danton!" I said astonished. "Married Gabrielle Charpentier?"

Phillipe nodded, then added thoughtfully, "I wouldn't want that face about my house."

I laughed at his predictable frankness, relieved to be reminded that some things were yet the same. "I agree," I said. Then I added, "But perhaps in time we shall grow used to him; after all it seems that Charpentier and his daughter certainly did."

CHAPTER 15

The next day I returned to St. Germain, this time not to wander but to sleep in one of the many alleyways I'd found the day before. By two o'clock I was well rested and heading for the boulevard, that part of Paris where two kinds of people gathered: those hungering for an audience and those demanding to be entertained.

By the time that I arrived, the day's activities were well underway. Here and there clusters of men and women collected, elbow to elbow, talking and gesturing wildly. Painted mimes and harlequins jumped out to startle me, and the fruit vendors and flower girls tried to stop me in the street. Relentlessly I pushed passed them all–the beggars, nobles, and *petite bourgeoisie,* until at last I stood before the theater.

''I'm glad to see you have taken up my offer,'' called Danton as he approached me.

''I've not decided yet,'' I warned him. ''I think you know my position. I can't trust just anyone. I want to know more about this man before I accept any proposals.''

''Of course, of course,'' he said. ''I'll tell you of him as we walk. His *cabinet* is just down the street.''

"I want to know before I go," I said.

"Come, he is waiting. I've told him of you–but not your circumstances. He cares to know neither. He's interested only in your work, and I assure you, Jacques," he said, seeing I still hesitated, "that Dr. Curtius's *cabinet* is a safer place for you than here on the street."

"All right," I said. "I'll go along, but I'll not make any decisions until I meet the man myself."

"Shall we go?" he asked, pointing out the way.

Reluctantly I followed.

"As I've already mentioned," Danton continued, "his name is Dr. Curtius, and it may cheer you to know that you are not the first 'unsavory' person to frequent his establishment. You need have little fear. But aside from that, all of Paris is in an uproar. Even if the authorities had the inclination, they wouldn't have the time to look for you."

"Uproar?" I said. "I've noticed nothing out of the ordinary."

"That's because you have not been to the cafés and clubs. I tell you plainly, Jacques, there is a revolution afoot." He said it with relish.

I stopped. "A revolution?"

"Oh, you've nothing to fear," he said, "for it is the artisans and peasants–the working people–that stand the most to gain."

"And what are we to gain?" I asked, making no effort to conceal my scorn.

He stared at me a moment, then said, "You shall know soon enough." Resuming his jocund air, he turned the conversation again to Dr. Curtius. "His waxworks have become the rage of Paris, for his figures are so lifelike that you almost expect them to speak to you while you gaze at them."

"They are full figures: life-size?"

"Most of them are. He does some busts as well, but they are less popular," he said.

"I've never done life-size figures before," I said.

''I told him that. Still, he could see by your medallion that you have potential, and he is willing to teach you.''

''I need a job, not a tutor,'' I said frankly, unwilling to think of any man aside from my father as my mentor.

''He will teach you as you work. Besides, even you must admit that there are things you've yet to learn. Ah, there it is.''

I followed his gaze to where a tall, lean black man dressed in oriental robes sat before an ornamental gate. Majestic in his finery, the man took no notice of our approach, but sat with a drum between his knees beating out a rhythm that kept pace with the rhythm of his speech. ''Come, come see the Master's *cabinet.* Come, come see the famous brought to life. Come, come see villains brought to justice. Come, come see the waxworks that delight. Come . . .'' His strange chant faded as we entered the inner courtyard.

The *cabinet* was a grand, two-storied apartment with a stone walk leading up to an enormous ornate door. The door was framed on either side by two large windows, each of which displayed numerous wax busts of popular Parisians–wealthy men, men like those that I had come to despise.

''I'm not impressed with those whom he chooses to display,'' I said.

''Nor is he,'' said Danton nonchalantly. ''It is good business to keep them there for now, but I assure you the doctor shall cast them aside when they fall from grace.''

''You speak as if you know when that will be,'' I said.

''Perhaps I do,'' he said as he opened the door and ushered me into a large, lavishly decorated room.

All about the room were tableaux of life-size figures arranged on Indian-carpeted platforms. Some were posed as if sitting for a portrait. Others were arranged about tables–some eating, some flirting, and some engaged in lively arguments. All that I had seen on the boulevard paled in comparison to Curtius's *cabinet.*

I was not permitted to gaze about undisturbed for long, however, for scarcely had my eyes come to rest on a grouping of well-dressed noblemen when one of them stepped forward. I jumped back, startled.

"I can fool anyone except Danton," said Dr. Curtius as he burst into a hearty laugh. Then, assuming a more businesslike air, he turned to Danton. "So this is Jacques," he said.

"It is," Danton replied, smiling upon me as if I were his prize.

Dr. Curtius then turned to me. "I've seen your work and it pleases me. What has Danton told you?"

"Only that you might have work for me."

"And that you are willing to teach him as he works," Danton added.

"That is so," said Dr. Curtius. "Have you ever worked with live models?" he asked.

"Yes," I said. "My father made me sketch from them for hours."

"How did a poor artisan get models?" he demanded.

I could feel my face redden at his question, but I tried hard to conceal the anger in my voice as I replied. "My father gave food to beggars and children who would sit for me."

"Then they were always living models?"

"Of course," I said. "What other kind are there?"

"The best kind–" he answered, "those that are dead. When you work only with the living you fail to see what lies beneath the flesh–the muscle, sinew, bone–all that gives life to what you see."

My expression must have revealed my distaste for his suggestion. "You are squeamish about working with cadavers?"

"I don't know," I said.

He stared at me for what seemed a long time. "You can put your mind at rest," he finally said. "I cannot get cadavers for my study here. I assure you, however, that I have no need of them for I have studied so many that the models I will use to teach you will provide vivid enough instruction."

''Dr. Curtius was trained as a surgeon,'' Danton explained.

''It was there that I began making my models of organs, limbs, whole skeletons,'' the doctor continued. ''My professors were astonished at my accuracy and soon began using my work for teaching.

''It was then,'' Danton interjected, ''that Dr. Curtius recognized his preference for molding rather than healing men.'' At this comment both men again broke into coarse, vulgar laughter.

''Come,'' said Curtius recovering himself. ''You have seen only what the casual observer sees. I will show you my most prized chamber, the chamber that my customers are willing to pay five extra *sous* to see.''

He led us across the room until we stood before an enormous gothic door. ''This was once a courtesan's drawing room–until now.'' He swung open the door. ''Now it is my Den of Thieves.''

He motioned me to enter, and as I did so, what I saw nearly took my breath away. Arrayed about the room were several gruesome scenes of torture.

''Here is where you see what lies beneath the flesh. Here is muscle, sinew, bone,'' said Dr. Curtius.

Danton stood by, a placid smile upon his face, as Dr. Curtius moved about the room, engrossed in what he considered his prize tour.

''This was Lescombert,'' he said pointing up to a woman hanging from a gallows. ''She murdered her husband, a most unwise thing to do.'' He moved past her. ''And over here we have the madman Damiens. You have heard of him? He tried to stab the King with a pocketknife.'' He stopped before the wax figure of man bound to a table, an executioner leaning over him, tearing at the guilty hand with a horrible pincerlike instrument.

He made his way about the room describing each crime and punishment with relish. ''Of course,'' he sighed at the conclusion of his speech, ''these executions were long ago, but there are still many in Paris who merit such rewards.''

''And there are yet many in Paris who would pay to see them get their just deserts,'' Danton added.

''Ah, that is true,'' Dr. Curtius agreed. ''That is why they love coming here. In this chamber every man can imagine his enemy upon the rack and himself as tormentor.''

The face of the Comte de Guiche's son rose up before me. I pushed him from my thoughts.

''Of course,'' Dr. Curtius continued, ''not everyone who comes into this chamber does so for the horror of it.''

''What other reason could there be?'' I asked bluntly.

''Well, it could help you learn more of human anatomy. It's not as good as studying a cadaver but there are certain advantages, don't you think?''

I did not answer.

''I also have a friend, Dr. Guillotin, who comes here frequently to study the instruments of torture.''

''And you do not see in that a curiosity for horror?'' I asked.

''Quite the contrary,'' Curtius replied. ''He believes that these instruments are far too brutal. He studies them merely to see how they work, for his dream is to invent a humane means of execution, one that will provide–in his words–'a clean, painless death for all.' And I think he may succeed. Still, I have warned him that Paris will not thank him for his efforts. As my coffers prove, the nature of man prefers not simple justice, but revenge.'' He smiled, then headed for the door. ''Come, we must discuss your place and duties in my *cabinet*.''

PART TWO
The Revolution in Earnest
1789-1793

CHAPTER 1
Summer, 1789

For the next year, my ''place'' was, for the most part, in the basement, and my duties were so numerous that I scarcely had time to sleep or to reflect on the fact that I was a fugitive in hiding.

I began each morning by attending anatomy classes with two or three other apprentices. Aside from the evening meal, this was the only time I spent upstairs, for the classes were held on the second floor in Dr. Curtius's study, a room which could best be described as both a wonder and a horror. What initially caught your eye when you entered were the many shelves lined with skulls, most of which served as perches for powdered wigs. Your gaze would then be drawn to the tables upon which were strewn models of hands and arms, legs and bodies. There was also a large cupboard in the corner. Its door was always open, revealing drawers filled with glass eyes, cheap jewelry, and strands of hair and netting. I soon learned, however, that these ''distractions'' were essential to our lessons.

Curtius was a master craftsman whose fame as an anatomist was known through all of Paris. But even without knowing of his fame, the lessons that he gave would have convinced me that he was unrivaled in this field. Although I cared little for the man and less for his art, I gleaned much from his medical knowledge. He was a hard taskmaster, and within weeks I had learned not only the purpose of every tendon, muscle, and joint but also the effects of movement, of aging, and even of disease upon the human form. My father had already bequeathed to me the greatest gift, the heart and eye of an artist, but my classes with Dr. Curtius made me better able to implement what my heart and eye conceived.

My afternoons were spent working in the basement, preparing figures for display. It was there that I met Anne Marie, Dr. Curtius's niece. She had but recently returned from Versailles, where for several months she had served both as a sculptor for and companion to King Louis's sister, Princess Elizabeth. In appearance she was frail and pallid, but the energy and intensity she put into her work were unequaled. She was exceedingly meticulous. If necessary, she would sit for hours repairing a minor flaw made by a less-skilled hand.

I remember clearly the night I recognized that she, not Dr. Curtius, was the one responsible for the "lifelikeness" of those who graced the *cabinet*. Those of us who were students not only worked but also slept in the basement. One night I awoke to see Anne Marie sitting at one of the tables, bent over the face of the *Dauphin*. Having been dissatisfied with the way an apprentice had done the young prince's eyebrows, she had returned when she thought we were all sleeping. With only one candle to work by, she was plucking out each brow and reinserting the hairs–one by one.

So intent was she upon her work that she did not notice that I'd awakened and was lying in the corner watching her. I continued to watch until at last she finished and slipped back up the stairs. I then got up and examined what she'd done. The *Dauphin's* brows had now the perfect arch and thickness. There would not be a beggar in Paris who would not now know the prince.

Yet as I gazed upon that face, I recognized something else as well. Despite all of Anne Marie's noble efforts, the face that I looked upon was no more than a shell; there was no soul to it. I had discovered that Anne Marie was the true artist of the family, but I could see as well that she could not fulfill her potential as an artist by working in her uncle's *cabinet*. I found myself wishing that I could take her back to my shop and show her how–with hammer, chisel, and stone–she could capture the strength of a man's character or that nuance of weakness that lay hidden in his heart. Wax was too artificial, too insistent upon reflecting only what the naked eye could see. I saw clearly that it was the medium of a mimic, not an artist. I went back to bed, troubled by the realization that as long as I was forced to work in Curtius's *cabinet* I could not fully enjoy the only solace left to me–my art.

* * *

I awoke the next morning in an ill humor and remained sullen throughout the day. I spoke to no one, and my mood and manner warned others that they had best not speak to me.

At six o'clock Dr. Curtius came down the stairs and to my disappointment announced, "All of you must be at dinner this evening. We are having guests."

I was in no mood to socialize. "I would like to be excused," I said.

"Not tonight, Jacques," Dr. Curtius said. "For Danton is among those who will dine with us, and he has asked specifically that you be there as well. He feels that the conversation may be of interest to you. Be cleaned up and in the dining room by seven o'clock." Before I could object further, he had disappeared back up the stairs.

I could think of nothing at the moment that Dr. Curtius, Danton, or anyone else might say that I would care to hear. Still, I knew I had no choice. Thus, I finished with my duties, cleaned up, and made my way upstairs.

The two other apprentices, Anne Marie, and Dr. Curtius were already there.

"Sit down," Dr. Curtius ordered as I entered. "I must greet our guests and bring them in."

I sat down next to Anne Marie. She seemed as loath as I to be there. "What's so important that we must be here?" I whispered to her.

"The men who are coming are the kind who insist upon an audience," she said.

"Who besides Danton?" I asked.

"Robespierre is the only other one worth noting," she remarked without enthusiasm. "He seems at first to be simply tedious, but the more you are with him the more distasteful his company becomes."

"Why?" I asked.

"You shall see." She had no time to say more, for Dr. Curtius had returned.

Six men came to dine with us that evening, but as Anne Marie had aptly observed, only two were worth noting. The others were but copies of either Danton or Robespierre. The two or three who kept close to Danton were like him, well-dressed but coarse men who ate, drank, and talked more like peasants than like *bourgeoisie*. But those who hung upon Robespierre were clean-shaven, scented men, as impeccable in manners as in appearance.

"Have you heard that the king has dismissed Necker?" announced one of Robespierre's men as soon as we'd begun to eat.

I knew that Necker, the Minister of Finance, was popular with the people.

"Necker?" bellowed Curtius. "Jacques, did you not just finish a bust of him."

"Yes," I said.

"And already he is in disgrace!" moaned Dr. Curtius.

"Only with the king," Danton said.

"From what I have heard," Robespierre interjected, "it is not the King who is displeased with him. It is Marie Antoinette."

"What shall happen to us now!" Dr. Curtius shouted. "France, it seems, is run by a woman–a foreign one at that!"

"The king is weak," said Danton. "And a weak king is no king at all."

"He may be weak, but he is yet strong enough to be dangerous," said Robespierre.

"Louis–dangerous?" Danton laughed. "We shall have him eating out of our hand before the summer's end."

"Don't be so sure," said Robespierre. "A man who has enjoyed absolute power does not easily relinquish it."

"That's just it," countered Danton. "Louis has never ruled absolutely, and he will soon submit to the people's demands. I tell you, before the summer's end we shall have a constitutional monarchy in France!"

Danton raised his glass, and several at the table cheered him, but before the cheers could die away, Robespierre added in his dry, almost mechanical tone, "Then how do you explain the military guards who have been ordered by the king into the streets of Paris?"

"Those guards will do nothing to oppose us," said Danton, but with less conviction than he had used heretofore.

"They shall never have the chance," said one of Robespierre's followers, "for Parisians everywhere are out tonight in search of arms."

"In search of arms?" I said. "Whatever for?"

"To defend themselves," said Robespierre. He turned to Danton and spoke as if to warn him. "It is rumored that the King has sent out the troops for the express purpose of cutting down those who would oppose him."

Danton paused. Growing very serious, he said, "It may be wise then for the lovers of liberty to make certain that all Parisians have the means to protect themselves from such a king."

Robespierre smiled knowingly but said nothing. I began to understand Anne Marie's assessment of the man.

"This is ridiculous," said Anne Marie with a temper I had never seen. "The King would never order his soldiers to attack the people of Paris!"

"You are simply too young and innocent to understand such villainy," remarked Robespierre.

"I understand Versailles better than any of you," she said, "for I have lived there."

"I can't believe it," Danton said with a laugh. "Little Anne Marie at court? Curtius, you never told me."

"She was sent there simply to do some waxworks for the Princess Elizabeth," Dr. Curtius explained.

"But I knew the King as well," she continued, "and I tell you he would never do his subjects harm."

Robespierre glared at Curtius, at Danton, and even for a moment at me. Then the glare vanished and was replaced by a condescending smile. "Not all of those at court see the political side of things. The king may well be both an admirable host and a devil of a politician."

"I tell you–" started Anne Marie.

"Enough!" Dr. Curtius's voice was threatening, and his niece knew–as did we all–that any further comment would be perilous. There was a moment of tense silence before Robespierre broke in to change the mood.

"It is amazing, isn't it," said Robespierre, smiling, "that Anne Marie could have spent time at Versailles and returned home without even the slightest taint of its corruption on her?"

His comment had the desired effect upon the doctor's temper. "She is a Curtius," he said.

By supper's end, the conversation had returned to more mundane subjects. As the guests made their departure, however, Danton pulled me aside. "It won't be long until you may again be able to walk about the city freely."

"Why? What do you mean?"

"I cannot say just now, but in a day or two–watch for me," he said.

CHAPTER 2

Danton's cryptic talk of freedom took away all hope of sleep. The following morning I was up long before dawn, bent over the fire, stirring up a fresh batch of molding wax that I would need for the day's casting. I could feel the beads of sweat forming on my forehead, for I'd been at the task for more than an hour. At last the wax was thinning. I reached for a bowl of turpentine and poured some in, then scooped up a handful of white and scarlet pigment. Moving my stirrer round and round, I let the colors fall, watching as the lifeless wax took on the tone and texture of a child's skin.

As I pulled the mixture from the brazier and set it on the stone hearth to cool, I heard someone coming down the stairs in haste. I looked up to see Dr. Curtius running toward me, his dressing gown, obviously thrown on in haste, flying out behind him as he ran.

"Jacques, hurry! I've received word that a mob has gathered. We must be quick," he said. "Come. Follow me."

I ran up the stairs behind him. Through the windows I saw that a crowd of men, who looked as if they'd had more drink than sleep, were milling through the outer gate and coming up the walk.

"Whatever do they want?" I asked the doctor, who now stood smoothing down his hair and wrapping his robe securely about him in a futile effort to prepare himself to receive the "guests."

"Let's find out," he said.

Flinging open the *cabinet* doors, he called to them, "Good citizens, you have caught us unprepared. It is too early for tours of the *cabinet* or for selling you our wares."

"We do not come to buy," an unkempt man said as he pushed himself to the front of the crowd. "Give us some heads!" he cried.

The crowd roared out in unison.

"What's mine is yours," Dr. Curtius called above the tumult. "Which heads do you prefer?"

"We want our heroes." one man cried. "Necker, Lafayette–"

"The Prince d'Orléans," another said.

Another cheer went up. Curtius turned quickly to me, and his smile vanished. "I know we have Lafayette and Necker. But the Duke–have you finished him?"

"I have," I said.

I saw a smile of relief replace the worried frown. "Well done, Jacques," he cried, fairly beaming now. "Keep them happy while I get those heads!"

I nearly panicked as I watched the doctor vanish, but as I turned around to face the mob, I saw Danton emerge. For the first time I was genuinely glad to see him.

"Citizens," he called out as he held up his hands. "I told you the good doctor was a patriot. We shall have what we have come for!"

As the crowd continued cheering, Danton stepped over the threshold and pulled me in. "A word with you," he said. "Your young friend–what is his name?"

"Phillipe, you mean?"

''Yes, Phillipe, that's it. Get him to come to me–at Charpentier's this afternoon.

''Why? What could you want with him?''

''I need someone to carry a message to the workers in St. Antoine.''

''What kind of message?'' I asked.

''It's nothing dangerous. I simply want him to spread the word that there is something planned for tomorrow. I want those in your neighborhood to have the knowledge–and to be prepared.''

I hesitated. ''I don't know,'' I said.

''Come, you must trust me,'' Danton hissed in a throaty whisper, ''for I tell you plainly that after tomorrow you will never need to fear imprisonment again. Tomorrow we shall storm the Bastille.''

''Storm the Bastille–''

''Lower your voice,'' he said. ''No one must know until I've had time to prepare key men, men like those in St. Antoine. They await my word. You will tell Phillipe?''

''You are sure there is no danger for him?''

''I am sure,'' he said.

''All right,'' I said.

''Tell him to come to Charpentier's this afternoon. And you–you be at the café early tomorrow morning–'' He broke off as Dr. Curtius came puffing up the stairs holding the three heads he had obviously had to wrench from their wax bodies. I ran across the room to help him as Danton turned and once again addressed the crowd.

''Here are your prizes,'' Danton said as he took Lafayette and the Duke from the doctor and tossed them into the crowd. Dr. Curtius, obviously relieved to see Danton and to hear the crowd's cheers of favor, stepped back inside and with a relieved sigh sat down on a velvet chair.

Danton took the head of Necker from me and tossed it into the crowd as well. Then, grabbing my arm, he pulled me back outside before the crowd. ''And here, good citizens, is the worthy artist of your heroes!'' Such cheering and applause rang out that I stood dumbfounded before them all. Danton leaned close and whispered in my ear, ''See how easily honor comes to those who will but take it by the throat? Yesterday you were an unknown fugitive; today I have made you a hero of the revolution.''

He turned back to the crowd again. ''Let us return to the cafés and drink to the revolution!''

''To the revolution!'' they cried out, and as a single organ, laughing and jeering, they made their way again into the street.

I stood watching until they were out of sight. I was relieved to see them go. And yet–strange as it may seem–I, who had but recently scorned my work in wax, was now filled with pride as I watched those very heads paraded as trophies through the streets.

CHAPTER 3

I arrived at Charpentier's by midmorning of July 14. The place was packed, for Danton was giving one of his orations. I scanned the room and saw Phillipe perched up on Charpentier's counter. I made my way over to him.

"I didn't expect to see you here today," I whispered.

"Danton said that you were coming, so I asked my mother if I could come as well. She said she'd let me if I made sure that you saw me home by evening. Of course, I told her that you would," he said smiling. Then he added seriously, "I don't see you half as often now that you live on the Boulevard. When will you be coming back to St. Antoine?"

"If Danton can be trusted," I confided, "I should be able to return soon."

Danton brought his speech to a rousing conclusion and stepped aside to give the floor to a pale, pathetic-looking man, but the cheering for Danton continued and was so enthusiastic that the second man was virtually ignored.

At length he leaped up on the table. "You have listened to the wisdom of Danton," he cried from the height of his newfound perch. "He has told you of the treachery of those in power;

he has told you of their cruelties! But what will you do with such knowledge? Will it fall as a dead man in the street?''

The crowd as one voice gave answer. ''No!''

''Let us right such wrongs! Let us cast aside all tyranny! And let us begin by setting the captives free! Who will lead us on our march to the Bastille?''

The noise in the café was deafening as the chants of ''Danton! Danton! Danton!'' rang out.

''I will lead you,'' Danton cried. ''But by my side shall be the maker of your heroes, the artist at Curtius's *cabinet* and a youth who but a year ago was held captive in that prison. His name is Jacques Chénier!''

The crowd took up my name and sang it with Danton's.

Phillipe, ecstatic at the praise I was receiving, climbed from the counter onto my back. Holding me tightly with one hand, he took his cap in the other and waved it in the air, yelling as he did so, ''Jacques Chénier!''

His action identified me clearly to those about the room and we were quickly swept to the head of the crowd, which now roared its approval.

''Let's waste no more time!'' Danton shouted. ''To the Bastille!''

''To the Bastille!'' the crowd echoed, surging through the door.

The crowd continued swelling as we passed street after street, and those of nearly every rank and occupation fell in step beside us. As we marched, pikes, clubs, and even guns were distributed through the crowd. I turned to inquire of Danton, whom I assumed would still be at my side. To my surprise, I found he'd vanished. It was I and the pale young man who now led the crowd. I began to feel uneasy.

Catching sight of the Bastille, I could see that others were already waiting for us at the gate. One of the men ran out to meet us. ''The raid on the Invalides this morning was successful,'' he said, addressing the pale young man. ''We have two cannons waiting just beyond the outer gate.''

"Good!" the young man said.

By now we'd reached the entrance, and emotions were at a fever pitch. But the crowd fell back as soon as they passed through the gate and saw what awaited them there. Three of the Bastille's cannons stood facing the ones they had set up, and another ten or fifteen could be seen poised above us on the towers. A silence fell, and many hesitated, growing more uncertain. But, of course, the young man at my side did not. "We demand to see the governor," he cried.

No one emerged from the fortress and the crowd began once again to gather strength. At length a deputy called out. "The governor will allow only two delegates in to see him."

The young man motioned two men forward. "Go in and take three of our militia with you," he ordered them. "See if Governor de Launay is willing to release the prisoners without incident."

The men entered and remained for more than two hours while the crowd, growing restless under the heat of an unrelenting summer sun, became obstinate in their demands for action.

Another messenger was dispatched, instructing the governor that he must relinquish guns and powder–and that a unit of our militia must be admitted without delay.

This messenger entered–and returned within moments. "Impossible!" came the governor's reply. A cannon roared, a musket fired, and the fight began.

I was unprepared for the pandemonium that erupted, and I fell to my knees as the surge of men and women stumbled over me. Fearing I'd be trampled, I thrashed about with all my strength and at last succeeded in getting to my feet, but I had lost Phillipe.

"Phillipe! Phillipe!" I called to him, but all that I could hear was the boom of the cannon, the crack of the muskets, and the cries of the dying.

Assuming that he had been swept with the crowd into the inner courtyard, I ran forward, dodging the swinging clubs and thrusting pikes as I did so. The shot of the muskets sprayed the ground around me, and the cannon kicked up so much dirt and debris that I was nearly blinded. Still, I stumbled on until I heard him calling, ''Jacques! Jacques!''

I moved toward the sound of his voice and at last saw him through the veil of smoke, crouched against one of the courtyard walls. I got to him just as the drawbridge began to fall.

Grasping my hand as tightly as he could, he looked up and asked, ''Are we going in?''

The crowds had blocked the gates. ''We have no choice!'' I said. It was then I thought of the *calottes*–and of Pierre. ''Come on,'' I said. ''I know a place where we may at least find space to breathe.''

We moved with the crowd across the drawbridge, but once inside, we were able to break away from the surge of humanity that headed toward the governor's quarters.

When the crowd had passed, I turned toward the towers, stopping only long enough to examine one of the guards who now lay dead.

''What are you doing?'' shouted Phillipe as I reached out my hand to touch the corpse.

''Looking for his keys,'' I said, pulling the the ring of cell keys from the dead man's pocket.

Taking Phillipe's hand again in mine, I made my way up the tower stairs.

''Jump up on my back and hold on tight,'' I ordered him, and he obeyed. Then, taking the stairs as fast as my legs could manage, I soon found myself outside Pierre-Joseph's cell.

''Climb down,'' I told Phillipe as I opened up the cell, ''and wait here a moment.''

I entered to see Pierre-Joseph at the table, sitting just as he had been that first night. He turned slowly to me. ''Jacques?''

''Yes, it's me,'' I said, glad that he had recognized me. ''I've come to take you out of here.''

He remained seated as before. ''What is the tumult? I have heard cannon and gunfire–''

''The Bastille has been taken.''

"Taken?" he said, now standing upright. "By whom?"

"By those–" I stopped to search for words. "By those tired of tyranny," I said, remembering the rhetoric I had heard of late. "Now come. I think we may now be able to make our way outside the gates."

"Where will we be going then?" he asked.

I paused, for I had really given no thought to where I would be taking him. "You will come home with me," I said. "That is–if you would like to."

He stood a moment more, weighing my offer, then gathered up his few belongings and followed me out the door. Phillipe stood waiting where I had left him.

"And who is this?" asked Pierre-Joseph with a joy in his face that I had not seen before.

"A friend of mine," I answered. "His name's Phillipe."

"You are very old," said Phillipe, staring up at my aged friend.

"Yes, I suppose I am," said Pierre-Joseph as he reached out and touched Phillipe."And you are very young."

Phillipe smiled back at him. "Yes, I suppose I am."

"Come on, Phillipe, up on my back again. I'll not take the chance of losing you a second time," I said. I hoisted him up and the three of us made our way back down the stairs.

I tried to prepare Pierre-Joseph for the possible danger we might face when we reached the lower levels and the courtyard. But the danger had passed, leaving only the frightful corpses of dead guards and citizens strewn about here and there.

When we crossed the drawbridge, the frenzied sound of the crowd made mad by bloodshed told us that the mob was still gathered in the streets. I hesitated.

"Perhaps we should wait," Pierre-Joseph said.

"No. I don't want to spend another moment in this place," I said decisively and barged through the outer gate.

I will never forget the sickening sight that greeted me. Just outside, a man, laughing as if he were possessed, danced before the crowd. In his hand he held a pike atop of which bobbed the governor's severed head. I stumbled back into Pierre-Joseph, but before I could retreat, Danton pulled me forward.

"Here he is! Jacques, my boy, we thought we'd lost you!"

It was then that Pierre-Joseph stepped forward. I could see Danton's eyes light up as he gazed on this ancient man. "Was this a prisoner?" He did not wait for my answer, but shoved me aside and pulled Pierre-Joseph to him. "Look, my friends!" he cried out to the crowd. "We may have released only seven prisoners this day, but one of them is the oldest captive in all of France!"

The crowd went wild, and before Pierre-Joseph could voice objection, Danton had lifted him up on the shoulders of two brawny men. "Let us celebrate!" he cried and swept my friend away. Phillipe and I could do no more than follow.

Pierre-Joseph was carried to Charpentier's café and celebrated as a hero. I could see, however, that the honor did not please him. Thus I made some excuse that would allow Phillipe and me to disentangle him from Danton and the admiring crowd.

"How disgraceful to be made–a–a relic!" he said in disgust once we were outside the shop.

"Come," I said, "they meant to do you honor."

He turned on me in anger for the first–and only–time. "Such men know nothing of honor! Do you call what we saw outside the Bastille tonight honorable? And they call me mad!"

"They have suffered wrongs," I said.

"Papa and Jacques suffered wrongs," Phillipe parroted in my defense.

"And so have I–for years," Pierre-Joseph said, "but I did not rejoice to see the Governor de Launay's head upon a pike."

"Nor did we," I said honestly.

"That is true," he said. "Come, bear with me. I am angered by such savagery. As for the honor those men meant to give me, you must see my point: they would have cheered a roasted pig as heartily as they cheered me if it had been lifted up before them by Danton.''

I shrugged, unwilling to admit openly that he was right.

His voice grew calm and quiet once again. ''Forgive me,'' he said. ''I have not yet thanked you two for freeing me from prison–or from that horrid man Danton.''

''He is rather horrid when you first get a look at him,'' said Phillipe, ''but you get used to him. You'll see. Right, Jacques?''

I did not answer but said instead, ''We'd best be getting home.'' The thought of St. Antoine at once lifted my spirits, and by the time we reached our street, I was in good humor.

''My shop is just two doors up from here,'' I told Pierre-Joseph when we had deposited Phillipe safely at his door.

''Are you sure that you do not mind my company?'' he asked, as we made our way down the alley.

''Not if you don't mind mine,'' I said, reaching for the door.

''You're a good friend, Jacques,'' he told me, ''and I will stay as long as I can do you good.''

His words puzzled me, for I could think of no ''good'' that such an old man could do for me. Still, I knew now that he was far from mad, and I hoped that he might prove pleasant company as well.

CHAPTER 4
Summer, 1790

By the summer of the following year, I had learned what "good" an "old man" could do for me. Indeed, despite his age he did far more for me than I for him. He washed the clothes, made the meals, and in the winter rose and had the fires burning long before I ever stirred. He also cleaned my tools, swept the shop, and kept my aprons mended. Besides these daily acts of kindness, he also opened both his mind and heart to me, sharing with me the knowledge he had gleaned as a youth at the University of Paris and the wisdom he'd acquired as a prisoner in the Bastille.

When he was not waiting on or talking with me, he enjoyed taking walks or sitting in the shop, reading aloud his treasured Book and playing his flute.

"Do you remember, Jacques, the first day that I played for you?" he asked me one day. He settled himself into his favorite chair, flute and Book in hand.

"Of course," I said.

"You know, little has changed since then," he mused.

''Surely you don't mean that,'' I said, looking up from my work. ''At least we are no longer prisoners.''

''Oh, I do not mean that our circumstances have not changed. Of course they have, but–'' he broke off. ''You remember what I said: that it is the heart, not the circumstances, that determines whether we are men of honor or disgrace.''

I nodded.

''Well, my heart is the same as it was that day. Is yours?''

''Mine is more content,'' I said. ''As a matter of fact, I think all of Paris is more content.''

''And to what do you attribute this newfound contentment?'' he asked.

''For one thing we are better fed, and the King has accepted the proposal of a constitutional monarchy. The revolution may have had a bloody start, but even you must admit that this past year has been relatively calm.''

''I fear it is simply a calm before the storm,'' he said.

''Admit it,'' I chided him good-naturedly; ''you just don't want to believe that Danton and those like him were right all along.''

''Hmmm,'' was all he said.

''I felt the same as you did when I first met Danton,'' I told him. I resumed my work, delicately chiseling away the last vestiges of unwanted stone. ''But he has done much for me and–''

''And you have grown used to him,'' Pierre-Joseph said.

''Yes,'' I said, without looking up. ''I have.''

The soft tapping of my tools was the only sound for several minutes, and I was grateful for it. At length, however, Pierre-Joseph broke the silence with a warning: ''Be careful, Jacques,'' he said. ''A man like Danton is not to be trusted.''

''He has done nothing to trouble me yet.''

''That is because you have proved profitable to him. But I tell you–'' He broke off, for he could see that I did not believe him.

"You tell me that all of Paris is content now that they are better fed. How about you, is that what has made you more content?"

"That–and the fact that I am making more money in a week than I could have made in an entire year before the revolution."

"And do you enjoy your work as much as you once did?" he asked.

"It is much the same," I said.

He laid his flute and Book aside and made his way over to one of my corner shelves. Taking down an old Rousseau my father had done, he turned it about in his hands, "This is marvelous workmanship–true art," he said.

"My father made that," I told him proudly.

"And this one?" he pointed to another on the shelf, a copy I made after studying my father's original.

"That one is mine," I said with equal pride.

"Then you have your father's hands, for they seem to me to be as one."

He saw the pleasure that his comment gave me. "Do you think that what you have there–" he said, pointing to the bit of stone before me, "is it as good?"

I looked down at my work. It was like many of the commissions I had done of late, a mere trinket carved from a stone that had been pried from the crumbling Bastille. "This is different. And besides," I added defensively, "this is what brings in all our profit."

"At what cost?" was all Pierre-Joseph said as he returned to his chair, picked up the Book, and opened it. "Shall I read to you?" he said.

I nodded, relieved to change the course of conversation.

Looking down he began to read:

> *When a great multitude had gathered, and they had come to Him from every city, He spoke by a parable: "A sower went out to sow his seed. And as he sowed, some fell by the wayside; and it was trampled down, and the birds of the air devoured it. Some fell on rock; and as soon as it*

sprang up, it withered away because it lacked moisture. And some fell among thorns, and the thorns sprang up with it and choked it. But others fell on good ground, sprang up, and yielded a crop a hundredfold.''

Then His disciples asked Him saying, ''What does this parable mean?''

And He said, ''The seed is the word of God.

Those by the wayside are the ones who hear; then the devil comes and takes away the word out of their hearts, lest they should believe and be saved.

''But the ones on the rock are those who, when they hear, receive the word with joy; and these have no root, who believe for a while and in time of temptation fall away.

''Now the ones that fell among thorns are those who, when they have heard, go out and are choked with the cares, riches, and pleasures of life, and bring no fruit to maturity.

''But the ones that fell on the good ground are those who, having heard the word with a noble and good heart, keep it and bear fruit with patience.''

''You notice,'' he said, as he laid aside the Book and picked up his flute, ''the difference was not in the word the sower sowed nor in the circumstances of those who heard, but in–''

''I know,'' I said. ''The difference was in how their hearts received it. Come, play for me while I finish up this work, for we haven't much time before we must be going.''

''Going?'' he said.

''Have you forgotten? Today is the anniversary of the fall of the Bastille. All of Paris is celebrating.''

''I am too old for celebrations,'' he said. ''Phillipe can keep you company. But I will play for you until you go.''

* * *

Phillipe and I reached the Champ-de-Mars by the Seine early in the afternoon. It was to be a magnificent celebration. A vast amphitheater had been excavated for the ceremonies and a temporary triumphal arch and altar had been built. When we arrived, men and women from every walk of life were awaiting the festivities, and it was not long before the rolling drums of the military could be heard in the distance.

"I can't see," Phillipe complained.

"Nor can I from here," I told him. "Let's move a bit farther down the river. It looks less crowded there."

We moved down to where the crowd thinned out, and though we had to wait a little longer, we at last caught sight of the parade as it came on.

"Let me up on your back for just a moment, Jacques!" Phillipe pleaded when he caught a glimpse of the military guards in blue, white, and red with guns and drums and banners waving.

"Only for a few moments," I said, letting him climb up. "You're growing like a weed and it's not easy anymore hauling you about," I teased him. "Soon you will be tall enough to see things for yourself."

Phillipe joined in the shouts of celebration which rose like waves washing over the marching guards as they came on. He was almost hoarse before all of them had passed to take their place in the hollow of the amphitheater.

After the parade, a mass was said in thanksgiving for the constitutional monarchy and the new era of freedom it had ushered in.

The mass was far less interesting than the parade had been, and many of the bystanders gathered in clusters to talk while the priest droned on.

"Look," said Phillipe, "over there's Latude."

I had not set eyes upon Latude since the day Thomas and I had seen him ride off in his carriage toward Charpentier's.

"He does not look pleased to be here," said Phillipe sullenly.

"I'm sure he's not," I said, my anger rising at the sight of him. "Men like him come merely out of duty. He shows his face here for fear that if he does not, he will be counted as a traitor."

''I would not call that a very good reason for coming, would you?'' I turned to see Danton standing at my side. Although Pierre-Joseph refused to go near Danton, I had seen him often over the course of the year, for I still frequented Charpentier's café and Curtius's *cabinet*. I found both were good for business.

''Nonetheless he's here,'' I replied.

''And we shall keep our eye on him,'' Danton assured me. ''By the way,'' he continued, ''Dr. Curtius told me that he sent word to Pierre-Joseph several months ago, asking him to come and sit for him, but he received no answer to the request. Why?''

''You would have to ask him,'' I said. ''He did not tell me anything about it.''

''To be cast in wax and displayed in Curtius's *cabinet* is no mean honor.''

''I doubt that Pierre-Joseph would agree,'' I said.

''You think not?'' Danton said. ''Well, I have heard some say he is mad.''

''No, he's not,'' Phillipe interjected.

''To refuse to be made into wax is hardly a symptom of madness,'' I said.

''You're right,'' Danton said, laughing. ''Still, Jacques, if he is your friend, you might encourage him to consent to a public appearance now and then. The people revere him now as much as they did a year ago, and it is unwise to scorn such admiration.''

The priest had finally finished and the crowd broke out in song; afterwards they began milling about again in search of better entertainment. I was about to take Phillipe and go when Danton stopped me.

''It is too early to go home,'' he said. ''And I have a good idea about how we can amuse ourselves.''

''How's that?'' I asked.

Danton looked down at Phillipe. ''How would you like me to teach Latude a lesson? For I know that it was because of him that your father had to go away. And since he may soon be coming home, we want to be sure Latude gives him no trouble.''

Phillipe looked up at me.

"Thomas need have no fear of Latude," I said. "It is the militia he must get past, for they are the ones who let no one who has been abroad back into Paris."

"It is for our safety," Danton said. "But even so, Phillipe's father would have been here now if Latude had not tried to cheat him."

"You're right there," I said.

"Come, let me show him a lesson," said Danton, encouraged by my agreement. "I promise you that he will be better for it."

I shrugged, and Danton at once took several strides through the crowd to collar the unsuspecting Latude.

"Citizens," Danton called out to anyone who would listen. "Here we have a squire turned patriot! Is that not so?" he said turning to Latude.

The captured Latude tried to maintain some semblance of respectability. He held himself upright and proclaimed, "It is true."

"Then you have seen the error of your ways?" Danton pressed him.

"I have," Latude confessed.

By this time quite a crowd had gathered.

"Well," Danton continued, as he moved Latude closer and closer to the river's edge, "I think it fitting that every convert should be baptized. What say you?" he shouted to the crowd, who cheered their affirmations back to him.

"Then Latude must at once be baptized!" he shouted and lifting up the squire, he dumped him into the river Seine.

Latude thrashed about wildly as the crowd looked on and jeered. He seemed to be desperately trying to make his way to the wharf but was having no success.

I had little sympathy for Latude but began to feel uneasy, for I did not want to think what Pierre-Joseph would say if this celebration ended as the revolution had begun–with death. But to my relief Danton spoke up again. "What say you, good citizens? Should I go in to see our convert does not drown?"

There were yeas and nays of equal fervor, but at last Danton jumped in. His enormous girth sent water splashing everywhere. Soon, however, he had Latude and was hauling him over to the wharf. As soon as the squire caught a few breaths, Danton again took hold of him. "Do you renounce your wealth?" he cried and dunked Latude, then brought him to the surface.

"I do," Latude sputtered, with no thought of respectability now.

"And do you give up your manor and all the goods therein?" Danton shouted and dunked him once again.

"I do!" Latude confessed.

"And finally! Do you renounce your lands, your dovecotes, and your hunting rights?"

"Yes!" Latude screamed before he could be put under.

"Then you are indeed a convert!" Danton cried, and he heaved the squire, exhausted, up onto the wharf.

"I shall draw up the papers and bring them to your manor house tomorrow," Danton announced, as he too came climbing out. Then, lifting Latude to his feet, he said, "I would suggest that you go home now."

Latude, though staggering, went off as fast as his weak legs could carry him. The crowd was laughing wildly, Phillipe and I among the rest. After all, I told myself, he lost only his possessions, not his life, and such a loss might indeed prove good for him.

"Come. Let's go, for it will soon be dark," I told Phillipe, and we both turned toward home. As we did, my gaze fell on the troubled waters that still splashed violently against the wharf. The vague longing that had come upon me during my quiet walk along the Seine stirred in my heart again, and with it, all amusement faded.

CHAPTER 5

Seeing Latude rekindled my anger and robbed me of the contentment the year of profit had brought forth. I again became restless, sullen, and even peevish toward Pierre-Joseph. He said nothing and continued to behave toward me in the same calm, steady manner that he always had. I thought once or twice of unburdening my heart to him, but my pride would not allow it. Besides, I knew what he would say, and knowing made me all the angrier.

Events came to a climax about two weeks after the Bastille's anniversary celebration. Phillipe, whom I had sent on an errand to Charpentier's, returned with a message for me: "Danton wants you to convince Pierre-Joseph to sit for you at Dr. Curtius's."

"Sit for me?" I asked.

"Yes," said Phillipe. "And Dr. Curtius has promised that he will pay you well if you will come and work for him again–just long enough to get a figure of Pierre-Joseph done for his display."

"Pierre-Joseph will not consent to it," I told him.

"He might if you asked him," Phillipe said. "They know he would never do it for anyone else, but he might for you."

''I could try,'' I said, musing on the money that was promised and the undoubted prestige that such a commission would bring. ''Yes. Go tell Danton that I will try. Why should he not consent to sit for me?'' I concluded.

Phillipe was running out with his message just as Pierre-Joseph was returning from his walk. ''And where are you off to in such a hurry?'' he asked Phillipe, who glanced at me and saw that I did not wish him to disclose his errand.

''Oh, just off–'' Phillipe said and hurried out.

''Look what I have,'' Pierre-Joseph said to me once Phillipe had disappeared.

I looked to see him holding a new, delicately carved flute.

''However did you get that?'' I asked.

''It is a gift from a friend,'' he told me, smiling broadly.

''A friend?'' I said, my tone betraying the slight I felt in not having been told of such a ''friend.''

''He is a very old friend. We went to the university together,'' Pierre-Joseph explained. ''I went to the Sorbonne a month or two ago, and there he was, shuffling about among the books.''

''He recognized you after all these years?'' I asked.

''He has changed less than I,'' Pierre-Joseph admitted. ''It was I who first recognized him. But it did not take him long to remember when I spoke to him. I've seen him many times since then; there is so much news to catch up on. You remember, Jacques,'' he continued, ''my telling you about someone bringing me an extra suit of clothes when at first they had imprisoned me?''

I nodded.

''I have found out that it was he. I have learned, too, that he tried more than once to bring me other things, but the guards would not allow it.'' He shook his head and a momentary sadness clouded his face but passed again as quickly as it came. ''Still, it is nice to know an old friend was remembering me, and it has been doubly good to renew his acquaintance once again. I imagine that those who see us at the Sorbonne must think it odd when they see two old, musty men laughing and remembering amidst the piles of old, musty manuscripts. Today when I arrived, he brought me this."

"It looks like an expensive gift," I said.

"It is valuable to be sure," he said, "for it cost him much in time. But not in money. He made it. He made one other for me, long ago when we were young. Of course, that one went the way of all my other goods the day I was imprisoned. I had showed him the one I'd so rudely carved, and today he offered to exchange it for this one."

"A good exchange I'd say."

"And so would I," he said, as he turned the new flute over in his hands, examining it proudly. Then, putting aside his memories, he brought his thoughts back to me. "And how is your work coming?"

"It could be better," I said.

"Is there anything that I can do to help?" he asked as he headed for his favorite corner.

"Yes," I said. "As a matter of fact there is."

He stopped. "And what is that?"

"I have just received a request from Dr. Curtius. He has asked me to come and do one more commission for him, one that will pay well in both money and future clientele."

"It sounds promising, but what can I do to help?"

"You can sit for me," I said.

I saw him stiffen in his chair. "Sit for you?"

"Yes. It seems that there is a demand for you as a display in Curtius's *cabinet,*" I said, not letting on that I knew he'd turned down such a request before.

"No," he said firmly.

"Why not?" I asked.

"I think you know why," he said quietly.

"No, I don't," I said. "Oh, I know that you do not like to be thrust in front of a crowd–as you were that night at Charpentier's. But this is not the same."

"And how is it different?"

"You shall sit for me in a quiet studio. There will be no thronging crowds. And I will do justice by you, you will see," I promised, imagining that I could easily win him over.

"I have never doubted your ability to do justice to any subject that you chose to do, but that has nothing to do with my reasons for refusing."

"Then what are your reasons?"

"Jacques, do you not see that to have people cheer and bow before me is something that is abhorrent to me? And for them to bow before a mere image of me is even worse. I have passed Curtius's *cabinet* on my walks, and I have seen how those poor, ignorant people gape and admire the images of those they call the heroes of their revolution. They are not heroes, Jacques; nor am I. I am an old, sinful man, but a man who trusts implicitly in the goodness and mercy God has provided for me through His Son. If they desire to worship, I would have them worship Christ."

"This has nothing to do with God," I shouted. "You are just being selfish. What of me? You may not want such honors, but they are profitable to an artist like me. Why can you not think of my honor rather than your own?"

"That is precisely what I am thinking of," he said calmly. "I would wish for you all the honor that faith in Christ would bestow upon you. And the immutable contentment that such faith would bring as well. But you refuse it."

"I want an honor that I can see, hear, feel right now!" I cried. "*That* would content me!"

"No," he said. "It would not."

"How would you know?"

"I know better than you think, Jacques," he said. "I know that there is a high price for the praise of men, and I know that once you have it, you must then live in constant fear of losing it–as one day you will. And when it is gone, there is nothing left, nothing but a cold and black despair."

''And money,'' I said. ''The honor that you spurn is what brings me clients, and clients are what bring in the money for our food, our wood, and every other thing. Or have you forgotten that?''

He said nothing.

I threw my tools aside and stomped toward the door. ''Eat what you like,'' I said. ''I will dine tonight at Charpentier's with friends.''

''Goodbye, Jacques,'' I heard him say with a tenderness that might have made me weep had I the heart for it. Instead, I simply slammed the door.

CHAPTER 6

I stayed away all that night and the next day as well. I did not care that my absence might cause Pierre-Joseph concern. I rather hoped it would, for I'd convinced myself that he had wronged me.

Before returning to the shop the next day, I forced myself to stop off at the Curtius's *cabinet* and inform him of Pierre-Joseph's stubborn refusal. I feared that since this was the second offer, Dr. Curtius would not take such a rejection kindly.

The doctor's warm welcome only increased my apprehension. ''I am sorry to have to tell you this,'' I began as soon as we were seated, ''but Pierre-Joseph simply will not consent to a sitting. I have tried–''

''Forget the old man,'' the doctor interjected. ''I've a better proposition for you.''

''You have?''

''Oh, yes,'' he said, growing more and more excited. ''Robespierre has consented to be part of my display. You know that he is fast becoming the rising star of the revolution.'' He leaned closer. ''He may yet surpass Danton, but don't tell Danton that I have said so. At any rate, I want you to do his figure! I tell you, Jacques, this revolution is good for business, is it not?''

''It is,'' I said. ''When would you like me to begin?''

''Two days from now. That should give you enough time to finish up any commissions you have now, for Danton and Charpentier have both told me that your popularity is growing.''

''Things are going better than they ever have,'' I admitted. Then, taking my leave, I promised to be back in two days' time.

As I made my way toward home, I thought on my new commission. I had seen little of Robespierre since that night when he and Danton had come to dine at Curtius's *cabinet,* but I had heard much of him. He had amassed quite a following, though I wondered how he'd managed. He was a small, weak-looking man, with a lifestyle that was so rigid that Parisians referred to him as ''The Incorruptible.'' In fact, he was the exact opposite of Danton. Perhaps that was why he had become popular; those repelled by the bombastic Danton were drawn to the rigid Robespierre. In any case, I knew that I no longer needed Pierre-Joseph's help.

By the time I'd reached St. Antoine, I had determined to tell Pierre-Joseph about Robespierre. I would let him know that his stubbornness had not diminished my chances of success. But at the same time I told myself I would assure him that, even if I could not understand his obstinacy, I could excuse it, and I would still do all I could for him.

I entered the shop, admiring myself for the benevolent stance I was taking toward my aged friend.

Oddly, he was not about when I arrived. It was past the time for his daily walking, and I knew that he rarely went upstairs before the evening meal.

''Pierre-Joseph,'' I called out, not really expecting him to answer. With a slight twinge of guilt, I wondered if he might have gone out looking for me. Then I noticed that on my worktable lay his Bible with a letter folded neatly underneath it.

I picked it up and opened it, feeling a vague sense of dread.

Dear Jacques,

I told you that I would stay as long as I could do you good. Well, I feel that time has passed. Do not misunderstand, however. I am not leaving because I am in any way angry with you. Indeed, I love you as a son. But I know that every young man must find his own way, and I believe it is time for you to find yours.

You need not worry about my welfare. I am leaving early this morning for England. That friend of mine, the one who made my flute, also assured me that I yet have property across the Channel. It is property that my family acquired many years ago when they left France.

I'm sure you may be wondering why they left without me, just as you have probably wondered why I did not tell you how I became imprisoned in the Bastille. The two stories are closely linked, and I have not told you either of them, not because I do not trust you, but because it shames me yet to think about them. But I now feel the time has come when my experience may be of use to you. Besides, as you would expect, I cannot say goodbye without leaving behind a good sound lecture for you. It is the prerogative–or habit–of the old to insist upon such things. But I know you will bear with me.

As I have watched you these past two years, I have grown to understand just how much you are as I once was. My family circumstances were much different, but my youthful heart was so very much like yours.

My forefathers were not artisans, but titled, wealthy men. In my lineage were great soldiers, scholars, and noblemen, men whose deeds in times past called forth the praise of kings. But they were also Protestant Huguenots, godly people who more than once were forced to choose between the honor of men and the praise of God. I know of only one who bears the name Aumônt–aside from myself–that chose men's praise over God's. Both of us have suffered for our folly. He was murdered in his bed on St. Bartholomew's Day in Paris in 1572. And I–as you know–was entombed in the Bastille.

But how came I to be there? During my years at the university, Protestants again began to suffer harassment from the Church of Rome. My father feared persecution–not for himself, but for my mother and my sisters, who were yet very young. He decided, therefore, to take them to England where they would be safe and where he could rear them as his conscience demanded. He begged me to go with them, but I was young and on the threshold of a promising career as a scholar and musician. I chose to stay behind. My father warned me that the day would come when the Protestants would again be forced either to renounce their faith or to suffer for it. I thought him foolish and I told him so. He did not rebuke me, but instead handed over his wealth and titles to me and assured me of his love and prayers. He also told me that as soon as they were settled, he would let me know their whereabouts and that if ever I had need of him, he would return without hesitation.

For more than a year, my life in Paris was all that I had hoped, but as you may guess, my father's predictions soon came true. At first, I was merely excluded from important social circles and denied prestigious posts. More than once my anger flared at such injustice, and I fought back, not just with words but also with my fists. It happened once too often. I was goaded into a fight with a young nobleman and beat him almost senseless. His father brought charges against me, but I was not especially fearful, for my wealth and rank were equal to his. I knew that in a court of law, I might be forced to pay some remuneration, but I thought I could afford it. What I did not know was that my adversary was also related to an influential bishop, a bishop who had the power to see that I–a Protestant–would never come to trial.

Two days before my scheduled hearing, I left the university and was on my way to send my father word of my predicament–just as a precaution. I was overtaken by the guards before I accomplished my mission. I was told that my wealth and titles would be confiscated and my family would never hear from me again. It grieves me even now to think of what they must have suffered, knowing only that I'd vanished and that the state now held their lands in France.

But God in His goodness saw to it that I had His Book about me when I was arrested. Under normal circumstances, I would not have had it with me, for I rarely read it much in those days. But a friend of mine had just returned it. He had wanted to examine how the French translation of the Scripture compared with his Latin Vulgate.

I remember the first night that I was left alone. The cell was a horror to one of my station. Trying to divert my thoughts, I opened God's Word and began to read at random. "Oh that you had heeded my commandments!" the passage began. "Then your peace would have been like a river, And your righteousness as the waves of the sea." Those few words awakened in me the full extent of my folly. I had tried to cast aside my godly heritage, but God in His mercy had not allowed it. I prayed that night to be forgiven for my sins and to receive the contentment that I now knew could come only from Christ. My prayers were answered, and I can say that although my years of imprisonment were far from comfortable, they were filled with a peace that surpasses human understanding.

So you see, Jacques, I do know what it is to be young and to be ambitious. I know as well the anger one can feel when he is forced to suffer at the hands of unjust men. But I have learned that through Christ I can rise above any of life's circumstances. It is this lesson that I want to leave with you, this lesson and my family's greatest treasure. You have been like a son to me, and as my son, you shall inherit it. Take care; my love and prayers are with you. And remember, if you should ever need me–for any trifling thing–my friend at the Sorbonne will know how to reach me. I shall return without the slightest hesitation.

Pierre-Joseph

My heart was yet unprepared to take in all the wisdom of his words, but I understood enough to know that I had been a fool to believe that he needed me. As I sat alone again in my shop, I knew that all along it had been I who needed him.

CHAPTER 7
Spring, 1792

More than once I toyed with the idea of visiting Pierre-Joseph's friend at the Sorbonne, but I was too ashamed to do so. What message could I send to Pierre-Joseph that would make up for the way I'd scorned him? No, I could not go to him. Nor could I bear to read the Book he had left behind, for each time that I opened it I thought of him, and such thoughts only made me more miserable.

Phillipe again became the only bright spot in my dismal existence, but he came less often to the shop. Thomas had at last managed, through Danton's help, to slip back into Paris, and he now insisted that Phillipe begin to learn a cabinetmaker's trade. Thus, each day that passed seemed only to increase my gloom. I found that even my work brought me little satisfaction.

As I struggled, so did Paris. Pierre-Joseph had been right: the peace following the fall of the Bastille was a deceptive calm. Paris was on the brink of a violent, raging storm, a storm that broke in all its fury when the king tried to flee Paris with his family. He had hoped to obtain refuge in one of the royalist provinces and there gain support for his tottering throne. But His Majesty's hopes were never realized, for a postmaster recognized the royal family and stopped them at Varennes. They were brought back to the Tuileries in Paris as royal captives. Men and women now spurned the idea of a constitutional monarchy and demanded the overthrow of the king. Some, like Robespierre, even began to insinuate that it would be wise if the king and queen were put to death. It is ironic that at the time the king's hopes were dashed, Dr. Guillotin's were realized.

"Have you heard?" cried Phillipe, dashing into the shop one afternoon. "There's to be no more gallows!"

I looked up at him.

"It's true," he said. "A man came into the shop today and said that the Paris deputies have at last listened to Dr. Guillotin. The poor as well as the rich can now simply have their heads cut off."

"That's good news, indeed," I said grimly.

"I say, Jacques," Phillipe chided. "Nothing cheers you anymore."

"I suppose I am bad company these days," I said.

"Not bad company," he said. "Just hard to cheer up."

"Try," I said. "Tell me what else you've learned. It seems that those who come to your shop are more talkative than those who come to mine."

"Well, according to gossip, Dr. Guillotin has a machine that can, as he puts it, 'separate the head from the body in less time than it takes to wink.' "

"That sounds like a bit of an exaggeration," I said.

"No, it's not," Phillipe assured me. "They say a surgeon has already tested it. He's cut off the heads of sheep, calves, and even corpses from the poorhouse. It works."

"Well, if it does, Dr. Curtius will be disappointed."

"Oh, I almost forgot," he said. "I had to run an errand for my father this morning, and while I was out, I stopped by Charpentier's. Danton was there, and he told me to tell you to stop by the *cabinet.* The doctor has another commission for you. He wants you to help him do a re-enactment of the first guillotine execution for his Den of Thieves.''

''He likes to plan ahead, doesn't he?'' I said.

Phillipe shrugged. ''He did say that he will pay you better for this one than for any you have done before.''

''Tell him when you see him next that I will think about it.''

''I think you ought to,'' said Phillipe, growing very serious.

''Why?'' I asked.

''I don't know,'' he said. ''It's just–well, when Danton gave the message, it seemed more like a command than a suggestion.''

''Are you afraid of Danton?'' I asked.

''A bit,'' he said. ''Papa is even a bit afraid of him, I think. I just don't think its wise to cross him.''

''You're not the first who has told me that,'' I said. ''Perhaps you're right. Besides, I've done so many commissions for him, one more won't hurt. And although I never cared much for that Den of Thieves, I think I might be able to stand working on it for a while.''

''Good,'' said Phillipe, relieved. ''And who knows, maybe the guillotine will never be used.''

''It will be used,'' I said.

And it was–within the week.

A forger named Pelletier was to be the guillotine's first victim. On the appointed day I accompanied Dr. Curtius to the Place de Grève, the traditional site of executions. But scarcely had the crowd gathered round before the thing was done. The amazing efficiency of the execution did not please the masses. They began to jeer the executioner and eventually to chant and even cheer, ''Give us back our gallows!''

''Did I not tell you that Paris would prove ungrateful?'' said Dr. Curtius as we turned to go. ''The nature of man does not crave justice, but revenge.''

''This will prove a poor exhibit then,'' I said.

''Oh, no,'' he assured me. ''We shall add a touch here and there. Before we are through, men will no longer look upon the guillotine as a humane instrument, but as an instrument of horror.''

CHAPTER 8

Dr. Curtius was right. It took me several months to complete the guillotine exhibit, but when it was finally unveiled, people not only flocked to see it but revelled in its violent composition. Soon after my exhibit opened, the king and queen were overthrown. Their demise unleashed in France a chaotic struggle for power. It was the Paris Commune, led by men like Danton and Robespierre, which emerged victorious from this political upheaval. To secure their power, these men instituted a special tribunal whose primary function was to round up, imprison, and eventually execute those suspected of once supporting the monarchy. Before summer's end, those same patrons who earlier frequented the *cabinet* were lining the streets to cheer as innocent men and women met their death by the guillotine.

In addition to the turmoil within the country, France was also embroiled in a war with Austria. By early September, news reached Paris that the enemy was closing in. In response, the Commune summoned "loyal patriots" to join the militia and defend the land. The call was answered by scores of men, but on the eve of their departure another crisis erupted. It was rumored that the imprisoned royalists were plotting to break free and restore Louis to his throne as soon as the militia had departed Paris.

Prominent members of the Commune were quick to act. Organizing those of us who were not part of the militia into armed bands, they ordered us into the prisons to unmask the counter-revolutionaries. We were instructed to try the prisoners. Of course, any who proved to be loyal citizens we could free. But those whom we found guilty were to be executed on the spot.

I set out with several others on the evening of September 2, assured that I was doing my civil duty and that I would be paid for the services I rendered. What followed was far from "civil," and I still shudder to think that I was offered pay for it.

We arrived at the first prison about nine o'clock that evening. I watched as prisoner after prisoner was hauled before our improvised court. It did not take long to see that these trials were a mere charade. Although a few prisoners were released, many more were executed, and as the night wore on, these armed bands of men–whipped up by rhetoric and fear–dispensed with the tribunals altogether. Those of us who opposed such a travesty of justice were afraid to protest for fear that we would be marked as royalist sympathizers. As we continued to break into cell after cell, I began hanging back, unwilling to partake in what was fast becoming wanton slaughter, but one burly man soon noticed my apprehension, "You, there, come out from hiding and see to that next cell," he said.

I felt I had no choice but to obey, and swinging open the cell door, I entered. Immediately my apprehension vanished, for there before me stood my father's murderer–the Comte de Guiche's older son. His father and his younger brother stood beside him.

"What do you want?" the indignant old Comte stepped forward and demanded.

I ignored him and turned my gaze upon his older son. I had grown much since he last saw me, so much in fact that I doubt he recognized me.

"What are you staring at?" he asked, and the tone of scorn in his voice sent me into abject rage.

I ran at him, and with the handle of my pike pressed against his throat, I pinned him to the wall. "You murderer!" I cried.

Out of the corner of my eye I saw his father move forward, but immediately I heard a voice behind me saying, ''No, you don't, old man.'' There was a moan and then a thud.

The young nobleman began struggling more violently, which only served to increase my blind fury. I held him fast and continued screaming–what, I don't remember. The next thing I knew, someone was pulling me back. ''Let him go, now. I've finished him!''

I stepped back and released my grip. To my surprise the young nobleman sank to the floor.

''I thrust him through for you,'' the man beside me said.

I turned and saw that the Comte de Guiche also lay dead.

Just then the Comte's younger son, who had been stunned to silence, found his voice and ran toward the man who'd murdered both his father and his brother.

''You've killed them!'' he screamed, beating his fists against the man's burly chest. The man thrust him away, and the boy, who was no more than thirteen, moved over to his dead father.

I saw him there–as I had been–so many years before. My fury melted, and I reached out to touch him.

In a flash of anger he thrust aside my hand. ''Get away from me!''

But hardly had he spoken the words before the man who finished off the other two, stepped up behind me and thrust his pike into the boy. ''That'll keep him quiet!'' he said.

''You fool!'' I yelled, turning on him. ''You–'' but he was gone, already heading for the next cell.

I took the boy up in my arms, intending to get help for him. But as I held him, I could feel the life blood flowing out of him. Help was useless now. I gently laid him down again, and as I did, I saw my bloodied hands.

''There's more down the way,'' another man called out to me as I staggered from the cell.

I stared at him a moment, then threw down my pike, turned, and walked away.

Once back home, I washed myself and put on a fresh suit of clothes, but the stench of death stayed with me. Though my hand had not actually performed the murders, I knew that the rage I felt against the Comte's son could well have killed him. As I sat alone that night in my darkened shop, I realized for the first time how much I'd become like those who cheered at executions.

CHAPTER 9

I sat in the shop all through the night. I was afraid to sleep, and it was not until the first sign of sunrise that I got up and moved about. Crossing to the shop window, I wondered if perhaps the light of morning might dispel the darkness of my spirit as it had dispelled the night. But my despair refused to leave me. Turning away, I wandered aimlessly about the shop.

At length my eye fell upon the Bible Pierre-Joseph had bequeathed to me. It lay upon the same shelf where stood my father's prized Rousseau. I took it down and began leafing through it. Eventually I picked a random passage and began to read. It was a parable about a king who desired to settle accounts with his servants. I thought it appropriate for such a time in France, and thus continued reading:

> *When he had begun to settle accounts, one was brought to him who owed him ten thousand talents. But as he was not able to pay, his master commanded that he be sold with his wife and children and all that he had, and that payment be made.*
>
> *The servant therefore fell down before him saying, "Master, have patience with me, and I will pay you all."*

Then the master of that servant was moved with compassion, released him, and forgave him the debt.

But that servant went out and found one of his fellow servants who owed him a hundred denarii; and he laid hands on him and took him by the throat, saying, "Pay me what you owe!"

So his fellow servant fell down at his feet and begged him saying, "Have patience with me, and I will pay you all." And he would not, but went and threw him into prison till he should pay the debt.

So when his fellow servants saw what he had done, they were very grieved, and came and told their master all that had been done. Then his master, after he had called him, said to him, "You wicked servant! I forgave you all that debt because you begged me. Should you not also have had compassion on your fellow servant, just as I had pity on you?"

By this time I no longer thought of the parable as an analogy to France. It was I who mirrored the unjust servant, and Pierre-Joseph the noble king. All that he had done for me came flooding back to mind–the simple acts of kindness, the willing gift of his great heart and mind. And I–I who gave but a few worthless "denarii," had held it up to him as if it were a debt. Worse still–I had demanded even more than money from others who had wronged me: I had demanded that they pay me with their life.

The letter that he'd left for me fell from its place inside the Book. Carefully I unfolded it and smoothed it out upon the work-table. The feel of it was somehow comforting. How I missed my wise, old friend! I could write to him, I thought. Yes, I could write and ask him to forgive me. It was not much, but it was a start.

I began to scan the contents of the letter, but scarcely had I begun when I was startled by a banging at the door. I looked up and through the window saw Danton, Curtius, and Charpentier. I got up and opened the door to them.

''Have you heard?'' said Danton, barging in. ''Robespierre is trying to have the king put to death.''

''From what I hear, the law forbids that,'' I said.

''Of course it does,'' Danton replied, pacing about in agitation.

''Robespierre's gaining influence, Jacques,'' Charpentier put in. ''I fear that he will win.''

''And we must be on the winning side with him,'' Danton said. ''That is why we've come here. There's something Dr. Curtius and I want you to do.''

''You see,'' Dr. Curtius endeavored to explain, ''if we are to beat Robespierre at his own game, we must do something even more spectacular.''

''I don't understand what you're driving at,'' I said.

''Robespierre is already pushing for the king's trial,'' Danton continued. ''Of course, to him that is a formality. He needs the Commune behind him if he is to pull the whole thing off–which I have no doubt he will.''

''Aye,'' added Charpentier, ''he's a sly one all right.''

''Not as sly as I am,'' Danton reminded him. ''At any rate, once the king's condemned, Robespierre will look like a hero. I must have a means of diversion that will bring the attention back to me. Curtius here came up with the perfect plan.''

''We shall do a wax of the beheaded king!''

''*You* shall do a wax of the king. I want no part of it.''

Danton stepped forward and grabbed my arm, ''What do you mean, you want no part of it? I have done enough for you. You owe me.''

''What I owe you is a guilty conscience,'' I said, boldly. ''Your Paris Commune not only authorized but ordered that charade last night.''

''Charade?'' Danton said.

''Yes,'' I replied. ''You told us it was our civic duty to ferret out a royalist plot, but those in the prisons were not plotting anything. They were waiting–waiting for trials, and for the chance to proclaim themselves as 'patriotic' as everyone else in France."

"You young fool," he jeered. "They were deceiving you."

"I am no fool, Danton. I saw young boys mowed down!"

"Young boys?" said Charpentier.

"That's right," I said. Turning to face Danton again, I added, "Pierre-Joseph warned me not to trust you."

"Did he now?" Danton replied.

"Come, Jacques," Charpentier pleaded. "You're being too hotheaded. Danton here didn't order the murder of young boys."

"Besides being hotheaded, you're being stupid," added Curtius. "Think of the money the figure of the agonized king will bring. And what should the king care if we make a profit on him? He'll be dead."

"No," I said. "I tell you I have had enough."

"Fine," Danton said in a calm but icy tone. "We'd best be going, gentlemen."

I watched them as they headed for the door, but just before they reached it, Danton turned. "That reminds me, Jacques. The loan I gave you."

"Loan?" I said.

"Yes. You remember. I commissioned that medallion from you and paid for it ahead of time. But by the time you finally brought it to me, I had no need of it. You remember that I had already won Gabrielle's heart by then, don't you, Charpentier?" he asked.

Charpentier nodded, as if perplexed at what Danton was driving at.

"At any rate," Danton continued, turning back to me, "I pulled your little friend aside and told him that I would give you a loan until you were on your feet again. You are on your feet again, aren't you?"

It took only a moment before I knew what he was up to: he was making a point. In truth, I owed him nothing; the money he had given Phillipe was not a loan, but he knew I could not prove it, for he had given it in secret. His charade now was to impress me with the fact that he could withdraw his aid as easily as he gave it. I determined that I would ''owe'' such a man nothing. ''Wait here,'' I said. ''My money's upstairs.''

When I came back down, I found Danton reading Pierre-Joseph's letter.

I walked over and snatched it from him. ''Do you always read another's personal mail?'' I snapped, and I thrust the money toward him.

''It rarely interests me,'' he said. ''But that–'' He pointed to the letter in my hand. ''I didn't know that old Pierre-Joseph was once a nobleman. That would interest those peasants and artisans who once revered him.''

''They would revere him still,'' I said.

''Perhaps,'' he said and turned to go. Dr. Curtius followed him out.

Charpentier lagged behind long enough to whisper, ''Be careful, Jacques. Danton is not a man to trifle with. I know.''

I spent the rest of the morning and the afternoon trying to decide what to do. I knew that Charpentier was right, and though I had spoken boldly to Danton, I no longer trusted myself to remain firm under severe pressure. If I stayed in Paris, I felt sure that he would find a way to bend me to his will. I would not have it! But the only way I could be sure that I'd escape him was if I fled from France.

I looked down at the letter I still clutched in my hand and remembered, ''If you need me–for any trifling thing. . . .'' I sat down and wrote to Pierre-Joseph.

My letter was not simply a plea for aid. I poured out my heart to my friend, confessing not only the failures of the revolution but my own as well. I told him of the king's overthrow and of Danton's and Robespierre's rise to power. I told him of my shame at having scorned him and of my murderous rage that night in the Comte de Guiche's cell. And, of course, I told him too of my discovery of Danton's self-serving cunning and of how he had discovered Pierre-Joseph's past. I told him everything, and it did me good to do so. Only then did I ask him if he could provide me safe passage across the Channel. I closed with the parable that I had read, and its effect upon me. I acknowledged that I had no right to ask anything of him. But I promised that if he could in good conscience aid me, I henceforth would do all I could to serve him, knowing that all the service I could render now would not repay my debt.

I delivered the letter to Pierre-Joseph's friend. Two weeks later, he summoned me to the Sorbonne and told me that Pierre-Joseph was on his way. I was to be ready and waiting outside the library at five o'clock the following afternoon.

CHAPTER 10

I packed up my tools, Pierre-Joseph's Bible, and a few belongings and was headed for the Sorbonne by four o'clock. When I arrived, Pierre-Joseph's friend was waiting.

"Where is he?" I asked.

"He is here," his old friend assured me, "but he wants you to go down to the wharf without delay. There is a seaman waiting. Here," he said, handing me a neatly wrapped cloth bundle. "I am to give this to you as well. Now go quickly."

"He will know where the boat is?"

The old man smiled. "He brought it here, did he not?"

"Of course," I said. "Thank you. Tell him I'll be waiting for him."

Within the hour I was at the wharf, looking for the seaman while keeping an eye out for Pierre-Joseph as well.

"You are Jacques?" a man behind me said.

I turned. "Yes–"

"Come. My boat is docked a bit further down."

As soon as we boarded, the seaman began untying the boat.

"You're not going just yet?" I asked him.

"We must," he said.

I grabbed the ropes from him. "But Pierre-Joseph–"

"Perhaps you'd better open that," he said, pointing to my bundle. Then he added, "Go down below. It is comfortable enough, and it's best if you stay there until we are out of port."

I released the ropes and went below.

Sitting down, I leaned myself against an old wooden barrel and opened the bundle. Out fell a packet of papers–and a letter. I took up the letter.

Dear Jacques,

As you must know by now, I am not coming with you. It is safer that way. You see, in the course of making arrangements for this trip, I learned that Danton knew of your plan to flee and that you had asked me for help. He made plans to insure that he could apprehend you as you fled, knowing that by catching you in "mid-flight" he could make fast his charge of treason against you.

I allowed his men to follow me yesterday as I completed my preparations for returning to England–preparations for myself, not for you. (The plans for your escape were all settled before I left home.) I believe that I convinced Danton's men that they were receiving the information about your escape that they sought. If events proceed as I hope, I will leave for England tomorrow. But just in case I am detained, you will find the deeds and titles to my property in England enclosed with this letter. Now that I've informed you of my plans, let me get on with more important matters.

I cannot tell you, Jacques, the joy your letter brought me! The grief you expressed assures me that God has answered my prayers and granted you one of His greatest gifts–the gift of godly sorrow, that sorrow which "worketh repentance leading to salvation." You now understand that the human heart is "deceitful above all things and desperately wicked," and now that you comprehend the heart of man, you are ready to learn about the heart and nature of God.

Let me assure you first that "the Lord is nigh unto those that are of a broken heart; and saveth such as be of a contrite spirit." God is now calling to you as clearly as he called to Isaiah: "Come now, let us reason together, though your sins be as scarlet, they shall be white as snow. Though they be red like crimson, they shall be as wool."

There is no need to despair over your sins. Your only need is to come to Christ, to believe in Him and in the Father who sent Him to provide atonement for you. You will find God true to His Word. In place of your wicked heart, He shall give you a heart of honor, one that reflects the righteousness of Christ. With such a heart, no circumstance can defeat you or rob you of your peace.

I will see you again—one way or another—but until I do, know that you are in my thoughts and always in my prayers.

Pierre-Joseph

I closed my eyes; the secret of the Seine had at last become clear to me.

EPILOGUE
Autumn, 1793

My time in England has proved to be rich and satisfying. The material wealth Pierre-Joseph bequeathed to me is more than I could have imagined. Still, such wealth is nothing compared to the spiritual legacy he provided. It is this legacy that has allowed me to drink of the Water of Life freely, and in my months away from France I have found that whosoever drinks of the water Christ gives will never thirst. For I know now that the water He gives becomes a fountain of water springing up into everlasting life. Pierre-Joseph not only knew of this fountain but, through much patience, brought me to drink from it as well.

My only sadness is that I will never have the chance in this life to share with him my heartfelt gratitude for such a gift. You see, Pierre-Joseph was never able to return to England. Although the people of Paris refused to allow Danton to imprison the revered survivor of the Bastille, they had no quarrel with his forcing Pierre-Joseph to remain in France. Before long, however, Danton was robbed of even this petty revenge. Within a month after my departure, Pierre-Joseph died peacefully in his old friend's bed. "His last thoughts were of you," his friend wrote, and in his letter he included Pierre-Joseph's parting words to me: "Tell him that even though I cannot come to him, I know that he will one day come to me. And tell him that I won't mind waiting."

Why then am I returning now to France? Well, I am told that Danton is fast falling out of favor. (He may soon find himself a wax in Curtius's *cabinet,* but not as one of the heroes.) Unfortunately, those who have known and associated with Danton, including Phillipe, his parents, and Charpentier, may soon be forced to suffer as well. My gratitude for Phillipe's enduring friendship would be reason enough for my return, but you may recall that I once made a promise to Charpentier as well, the promise that I would not forget him. There is but little time to keep such promises and to provide those I love a way of escape. Thus I return, and I have peace that God will reward my journey. Indeed, it is He who sends me. If those I love must die, they shall die in Christ.

If, however, God sees fit to grant my friends and me a safe return to England, I will rejoice in my renewed fellowship with them. I especially look forward to those times that Phillipe and I will share. I hope one day to sit with him in the corner of my drawing room, with the bust I have made of Pierre-Joseph beside us on the mantel, and I will read to him as my old friend once read to me. The bust? Yes, I have made a bust of Pierre-Joseph. It is in stone, and I assure you that he would not object to this one, for I did not trust in only my artistry to reveal his noble soul. At the base of the sculpture is inscribed his attitude and mine concerning "images":

If you desire to worship, worship Christ.

AUTHOR'S NOTE

Although the three principal characters in this story–Jacques, Phillipe, and Pierre-Joseph–are fictional, there are several historical figures included as well. Danton, Robespierre, Charpentier, Dr. Guillotin, and Dr. Curtius and his niece are all people of history. The individual influence of these historical figures on the events of the Revolution varies greatly. Danton and Robespierre were driving political forces; and Dr. Guillotin, through his invention, unwittingly became the Revolution's symbol of terror. Of less historical significance are Charpentier, Dr. Curtius, and his niece. These characters are nonetheless intriguing. Charpentier's café was a popular gathering place for patriots, as was the Curtius *cabinet.* It is interesting to note that today's French cafés are still buzzing with conversations on politics and philosophy; and although the popularity of Curtius's *cabinet* has died out in France, it continues across the channel. After the Revolution, the doctor's niece, Anne Marie, married and settled in England, where she opened her own museum of waxworks. This museum, still popular today, is known as the famous Madame Tussaud's.

The triumphs and tragedies of the French Revolution are myriad, and like all revolutions, this one had both heroes and villains. The purpose of this story, however, is not to revere or to disparage any specific historical idea or personality; rather it is to show that regardless of time, place, or circumstance, the essence of true honor is the same.